The

Crucible

of

Achilles

By Takis John Pepe

Acknowledgements

The most concise acknowledgement is achieved in thanking God, who moved me to write this and orchestrated my life and the people in it to facilitate the act.

THIS MEANS YOU!

Foreword

"The Trojan war is the original source of so many of our cultural expectations of soldiers, of literature, of human behavior and of the interplay between the divine and the mundane. So much of our cultural tradition originates in the Trojan War that we continue to value it, even unconsciously, as the source of the archetypes for which we model our behavior."

Brig. General John S. Brown

United States Army

Homer, the Greek poet and author, blind and illiterate, is credited as the father of the first and oldest works of Western literature, that of the *Iliad* and the *Odyssey*. It is rumored that he lived 2,500 years ago in Smyrna, a modern city about a five hour car ride south of the archeological remains of Troy in what is now part of western Turkey. He would have dictated his epics about 500 years after the fall of that once fabled city.

The Homeric Question is an ongoing scholarly debate about the veracity of the *Iliad* as conveyed through an oral tradition which no longer exists. The existence of the man himself is far from certain, yet most agree that his tale was likely rooted in a real event. In fact, it was probably not his story at all, but rather a history he learned from a singing poet before him and another before him, all going back to the actual war.

In the 1930's, a man named Millman Parry traveled across regions of Bosnia and Yugoslavia where oral tradition was common and literacy was rare. The result of his findings was that oral tradition can and has preserved historical events with a high degree of accuracy, even across many centuries.

The *Iliad* would have survived half a millennia of oral tradition before its last verbal incantation was preserved in the very first Greek letters. It is believed that this alphabet was invented for the sole purpose of recording Homer's epics, and that these texts were then used for scholarly reference when teaching others to read and write.

So did Achilles actually exist? On an academic level, it is impossible to say. Even Parry recognized that while the essential facts of an event may persevere an oral tradition, each singer likely embellished and added elements to the story, particularly to the characters.

I contend, that just as the epics are not a product

of one singer, but rather many singers, so too is it possible that Achilles was likely an effigy of many men…of many heroes.

So often we wonder where these great men have gone, not recognizing they still live in our blood and breath. It is only the battles and enemies that have changed. In my story, you will again find the formidable Hector, the beautiful Briseis, the avaricious Agamemnon, the dastardly Paris…and the brave Achilles, all reborn in their contemporized forms. Even the Greek Gods of old, ever present in the original text, have been given their modern equivalent. It is here I know I risk alienating the agnostic readers, but I urge them to view the Christian references the same way they would the mythological gods of the ancient text. To those of faith who may have different views, I hope you can at least appreciate the, at times, unorthodox exploration into divinity.

CHAPTER ONE

The music and jeers of a belligerent crowd reverberated through the shady nightclub walls and landed, only somewhat dampened, in the cramped storage room filled with amateur cage fighters. The booming, albeit muffled voice of the announcer, only added to the tense atmosphere which resembled gladiators readying for battle in the pit beneath the Colosseum. Some were already perspiring in nervous anticipation as they stretched, shadow boxed or wrapped their hands in preparation. Others, having already fought and lost, treated minor injuries or sulked in the corner.

The victorious were not present. They were savoring their short lived triumph and momentary celebrity at the bar. They did not dare return to the makeshift locker room for even a moment to change out of their bloody fight shorts or unwrap their swollen fists.

These items served as their special identifiers, encouraging the tipsy girls to smile their way or the drunkards to approach them in admiration for a pat on the back or shake of the hand. No, they knew if they came back to the locker room to clean up they would emerge only to vanish in the crowd that just a moment before cheered so passionately for them.

ACHILLES

Archie had a different pre-fight ritual. He straddled a punching bag which lay on the floor, carefully writing, "Diane" on the inside of his muscular forearm in black marker. He finished the inscription and pulled the open fingered MMA style gloves over his wrapped and taped hands, flexing his fingers and testing the fit by punching his palms. Archie possessed a bearing and countenance beyond his 27 years which showed now in his comparative calmness. Somewhat short by ideal standards and always joked that when it came to being tall, dark and handsome, "Two out of three ain't bad." Indeed, he was dark and handsome with rugged, ethnic looks that nearly screamed *Greek* with his sandy hair, copious stubble and olive skin. If there were any doubt to his ancestry, emblazoned on his sculpted bicep was a simple black ink tattoo of a helmeted ancient Greek warrior in profile. He also held a sadness evident in his dark eyes though it was seldom seen by others since he hid it behind a charming smile whenever he spoke.

That sadness was there presently as he stared pensive into space but pulling his usual trick, he banished it with a quick smile as his manager and best friend entered the room.

PATROCLUS

Byron stepped over a defeated fighter sprawled on the floor with his feet on a mop bucket and a cold beer in his bruised eye socket. Then he stood wordlessly over Archie a moment, sizing him up. Byron was only in his mid-thirties but had been managing fighters since he retired from the cage himself half a decade ago. In that time he had developed a keen eye for evaluating a fighter's mental state by simply looking at him for a few seconds. With Archie, he could do it in even less time, so well did they know each other.

Byron took one final drag from his cigarette before tossing it in the mop bucket between the propped up feet. Kneeling, he doffed his tired wool flat cap so he could touch his forehead to Archie's in what must have been a familiar custom as the two embraced each other by the neck like tired boxers in a clench.

Byron whispered, "Blessed be the Lord, my rock, who trains my hands for war and my fingers for battle." Archie smiled softly at the familiar, Marlboro scented psalm. Then Bryon spoke more casually as though to a close friend, "God, be with Archie tonight as he fights in your name and in your honor. Be his shield and buckler and let Your will be done. Amen." Archie echoed his own "Amen" as Byron rose.

As Archie rose, Byron pulled his hat back down on his head and took Archie's gloved fists, inspecting them as he spoke. "He's tall, Archie. Long arms…like rakes. He's gonna have some reach on you."

"That's about all we know about him?"

"Sorry, brother. You know how it is fighting in a place like this. We ain't gonna to get stats on these guys like in a sanctioned gig," Bryon said, slapping each gloved fist with his palm as though it were a stamp of approval.

"Don't I know it. I'd take the sanctioned fights if they only paid a damn," Archie spat out between a few loose warm up punches.

Byron sighed. It was never his idea to have his guys fight illegal bouts in the seedy bowels of the

Rock's nightclub. That was never what he wanted, but his boys needed cash and the club was paying them well enough. Hell, he had refused when Archie first proposed the idea. And they came to fight anyways. In fact, they had followed Archie's lead as they usually did. Bryon came that first night only as a reluctant spectator, but something happened after the bell rang and Archie went to it. He felt it start in his chest and permeate his being. As the bell rang signaling the end of the first round, Bryon fought through the crowd to get to the cage, to get to Archie. And when Archie saw Bryon he brushed aside the corner men the club provided to cling to the cage to be near him. And then it was just the two of them. The belligerent crowd threatening to heave Byron aside was lost as he coached Archie through that metal fencing. And to see Archie follow through on his instruction and win in the next round….there was just no turning back. The Rock's was as far from a church as you could get and yet Bryon knew that unlikely place was exactly where God wanted him.

Byron looked at Archie in consternation. "Well, all I want on your mind right now is getting around that reach. You know how. We've trained for it. Don't waltz with him if you can help it. Take him to the mat first chance you get and keep him there. God will do the rest."

Archie nodded his reply as he stepped past Bryon and jogged up the short staircase that led to the back stage area. He waited behind a theatre curtain that hid him from the crowd in the club. He was near the base of the disc jockey pulpit and he glanced up at the pale DJ spinning records and whipping his ginger locks to the rhythm of his own beats. When he saw Archie, he flashed him a five finger signal which Archie understood to mean he was on in five minutes.

He shoved his mouthpiece in and bit

begrudgingly down on the thick rubber, breathing through his nose which the contraption forced him to do. He hated wearing the damn thing, but he also enjoyed a frequent smile and occasional steak. It was a cheap price to pay, far more affordable than the dentist. Besides, he knew once the fists started flying that mouthpiece would vanish from his mind. He used to gripe inwardly in the same way before patrols in Iraq and Afghanistan. It was a ceremony he loathed, strapping on the heavy Kevlar helmet and flak vest which weighed him down like a lead straightjacket…and yet when the bullets started flying he would always feel terribly nude and exposed like a tooth stripped of its enamel. The enemy would open up and his instinct was to find cover, desperately and quickly like Adam and Eve the day they discovered their nakedness. Then the two thick steel plates between which his heart beat felt like mere scraps of silk sheen.

On the opposite side of the stage a tall fighter

stepped out with a blonde crew cut and too many tattoos for most employers to hire. Archie knew this was his opponent and sized him up accordingly. He had long limbs, as Byron had said. Archie sighed. Long limbs meant he would have to take a few hits to get inside his range where he could do some damage himself...or grapple this guy and take him down to the mat. Down there, Archie would neutralize the advantage his opponent had in those long legs and arms and win by submission. That meant Archie could strangle him until he passed out or tapped the mat in surrender. Or Archie could win by twisting some appendage into an unnatural position, teasing a joint or bone to the point of breaking until this guy quit. Much of Archie's strategy was to study how the human body worked and moved so he could manipulate it into a position that it did not work and thus would break. Yes, that would be his plan of attack. Archie would turn the great length of his opponent's arms against him by leveraging them against their own joints, like calcium fulcrums.

Of course, he knew all too well that plan could go out the window, but he had learned the value of planning in Iraq. Then it took place nearly every moment for hours before a convoy mission, leaving the men no time to consider the terrifying odds of the gambit they were about to embark on.

There was only one last thing to do. Archie dropped to one knee to say a quick prayer. It wasn't that Bryon's prayer didn't count but Archie didn't feel his own was redundant either. Archie asked for the added measure that nobody leaves the cage broken or hurt beyond recovery before crossing himself. Noticing this moment of piety, his opponent shouted from across the stage, "Better pray for a fuck'n miracle!"

"I'm praying for you too, asshole," Archie said, his retort muzzled by the mouthpiece like a plastic bit.

Cued by his requested AC/DC track pounding over the crowd, he stepped beyond the curtain.

The cage stood before him, a pentagon of black fencing and empty blue mat, the only vacant space in the otherwise bursting club. The patrons pushed against the cage, embracing it as a collective, while still more were screaming from their second floor perch. It was one of the last fights of the night at almost two in the morning and this mob was enriched with the hours of heavy boozing. Their aggression was palpable, galvanized by the display of violent sport they were nearly immersed in themselves. At this late hour, the men in attendance were starting to feel cheated as it became clear their ambitions of a one night stand were likely to go unfulfilled. The only suitable recompense to assuage their frustration was a brawl of their own, so they passively aggressively sought each other out while the women they had been pursuing paid them no mind on their way to the bathroom to liquidate the night of free drinks.

Ah, yes, the women. Archie grinned at the thought and spit his mouth piece out and tucked it behind his ear so he could smile. He flexed his biceps and kissed each one in an overt display of bravado as he moved toward the cage. Archie wore his ego as brilliant, golden armor and saw nothing around him which could dent it. It was this shining boldness which made others envious and hostile towards him, such that they sought to strip him of it as though they could take it to don themselves. If not for this dazzling buckler, his personality, his very soul manifested, would have been destroyed years ago by a world hell bent on destroying all divinity, even that miniscule amount which all men carried in their hearts.

The door was held open by the tattoo sleeves of Mackey who shook his head in an attempt to hide the sly grin behind his fiery, red beard.

ODYSSEUS

While not much older than him in years, he surpassed Archie in cleverness, tackling problems often in a less direct manner. A potato farmer's son from Ireland, he had learned to coax the resilient vegetable from stubborn soil. He left his country a few years before to chase a fighting career, but the pursuit had taught him that the fight not fought was the surest victory. As his passion for the sport diminished, his love for all he had left behind grew. His father's land seemed to call from across the seas that separated them. Moreover, he had left his high school sweetheart behind, a beautiful girl who, by now, was an irresistible woman. His desire to return home was made all the more urgent by his innate knowledge of men who he knew could not simply admire such a beauty. They would be possessed to possess her, moved by human conquest. He was only the cost of a plane ticket away now, a sum he mounted by plying his cunning as a corner man.

He offered, "Get in close, or stay away. That's what I'd do. He has some serious reach...arms like a fucking orangutan."

"Maybe I should have brought some bananas," Archie replied, attempting to ruffle Mackey's finely manicured hair as he slipped past and into the cage.

"Yeah, well, this place ain't far from being a zoo," Mackey grumbled, stooping to pick up a tin bucket crammed with a towel, water and other tools of the corner man. Archie trotted around the perimeter of the octagon, running his hand along the fencing and against the fingers the crowd rammed though. Half way around, he high-fived the announcer who belted into a cordless microphone, "A local fighter out of our own Wilmington, North Carolina, he fights out of the Upper

Room Praise and Worship Church, standing five foot eight inches, he comes in at a lean, mean, 155 pounds. Let's make some noise for . . . T.N.T---!"

Archie grinned from ear to ear at the ensuing roar as he completed his lap, coming back full circle to meet Byron and Mackey. Archie was blowing a kiss to a woman with full grown breasts pressed inside of a child-sized shirt, when Byron slapped a dab of Vaseline on his forehead. The jelly had two purposes: One was to glide the gloves of the other fighter over the skin, instead of catching the flesh and cutting. The other was to refocus Archie to swinging fists rather than swaying breasts. Bryon spoke as he expertly spread the Vaseline over Archie's brow and cheek bones. "Ok, Big Sexy, fight now, flirt later. You're a fighter not a stripper. Remember, breathe with each punch you throw. Don't lose your form and keep your composure. Okay, brother?"

Archie nodded affirmative as particularly harsh rap lyrics blared from the club's sound system with enough force to rattle the cage. His opponent stepped onto the stage, eyes deathly serious and already set in his direction.

The announcer bent backwards as though the microphone was pushing him, but fought it back with his booming voice to regain an upright position. "Coming in at 167 pounds, he is stacked at sex feet and fighting out of Carolina Beach's Gladiator MMA. Get ready for Carl the Machine Sheed---!"

"167, my arse. I saw him fight last week at 190! The liars. Just look how much weight he's got on you," Mackey remarked in disgust as Carl stepped slowly and deliberately past them, staring them down on his way.

Archie shrugged it off. "What? Are you worried the paramedics won't be able to carry him out of here?"

The referee stumbled into the cage led by a tilted

beer bottle pressed against his lips. A squat, balding man in sweat pants and a dirty shirt, he finished his beer to the last drop and then leaned over the side of the cage to hand the empty vessel to a passing cocktail waitress. Bryon studied the drunken referee a moment and then tapped Archie on the shoulder. "I had a little chat with our referee. There won't be any of that funny business that went on last week. Everybody will play by the rules tonight."

"As if this place has rules," Mackey spurned as he helped Archie out of his desert tan t-shirt, a remnant of his enlisted uniform which was still serving its purpose in battle. Bryon knocked his knuckles on Archie's athletic cup to ensure its placement and double checked his gloves. Then he seized Archie in an embrace and said, "All right, brother. This is it. We have done everything we could do to be ready. Now just let it rip."

When he broke, Mackey snared in him in a similar

hug. "Get in close or keep away, you crazy, Greek asshole."

Archie chuckled, "Eh, go get a drink you mic bastard."

The cage was cleared of all except the drunk referee and the two hungry brutes who were vying for a victory that could not be shared nor attained without the other's abuse. The spectators hushed in excitement and those patrons at the bar charged with drink in hand to join the swarm around the cage. The referee, with as much ceremony as he could muster, took center stage and pointed a hairy arm at Carl. "Are you ready?"

Carl replied by swatting the air with a few quick jabs and a solemn nod. The referee whirled in Archie's direction and began again, "Are you read..." He trailed off gazing at Archie who was seemingly oblivious to the impending fight, on bended knee and sweet talking the beaming ring girl through the cage. Grumbling, he sauntered over to the preoccupied fighter, grabbing him by the forearm and yanking him to his feet. Archie flashed the girl one last smile with a, "call me" hand pressed to his head as he was tugged away.

The referee once more assumed center stage to jerk his arm in the air and yell, "Fight!"

A dinging bell echoed his proclamation which Archie and Carl obeyed, drawing closer in swirling circles. Seeing an opportunity to catch Carl and take him to the mat as planned, Archie lunged for the taller fighter's hip, but Carl was able to move out of Archie's range with a great stride backwards. Before Archie could reposition himself, Carl followed up with a wild uppercut, a heavy fist on a fully outstretched arm which caught Archie under the chin. Archie's head was tossed back with so much force his mouthpiece slipped from his jaw and flew over the top of the cage, landing with a splash in a bar-goer's drink.

Some of the crowd cheered at the spectacular violence, but others jeered and booed at the evidently rapid conclusion of the fight as Archie stumbled back, clearly hurt. They felt the cost of their entry fee entitled them to a more protracted bloodshed.

Carl threw himself on Archie's back, seizing his opponent from any retreat and tumbling them upon the mat. Clasping Archie's neck between his forearm and bicep, Carl ratcheted tight the rear naked choke .

The blow had stunned Archie, but now that the weight was off his wobbling knees, he felt reassured. Carl nearly had the choke set, but Archie had a few fingers between his adversary's forearm and his own neck. He used these to pry the pressure from the left side of his windpipe. The rear naked choke was a blood constricting hold which when fully applied, would result in blood deprivation to the brain causing unconsciousness in twenty seconds or less. Archie could feel that Carl had successfully clamped his right carotid artery and could no longer hear even the raucous crowd over the thudding of his heartbeat in his ear drums.

Despite the precariousness of his current situation, Archie remained level headed. His trachea was unburdened so he breathed deeply, feeling the strength return to his legs that the upper cut had robbed him of.

Byron rushed to the cage to be by Archie's side. His face was only inches from Archie's but he screamed to be heard over the roar of the crowd and release his own dose of adrenaline, "Turn away from the choke, Arch! Turn away from it!"

Archie peered up from Carl's constricting clutch, flashing Byron his best wink and smile with blood stained teeth.

"Don't look at me!" Byron admonished, shocked by his own fighter's persistent bravado.

What Archie did next was considered impossible

in the world of mixed martial arts. He grasped Carl's forearms and working against the principals of leverage that made the choke formidable, he pried them apart in a Herculean feat that defied the teachings of Brazilian Jiu Jitsu. The crowd convulsed like a hyperventilating lung at this dramatic turn of events, spittle and oaths flying from their drunk mouths.

Before either fighter could recover to their feet, a beer bottle shattered across the mat. It was hurled from the second floor balcony by a frustrated spectator who had bet against Archie

The two fighters, unsure how to proceed so near the shards. Archie shook his head in mock disapproval, "Alcohol abuse."

Pulling a dirty rag from his belt, the referee fell to his knees to sop up the mess. He gave the fighters an annoyed glance. "You fuckers go on and fight! I got this!"

Archie shrugged but didn't miss a beat as he felt Carl scramble beneath him. Snatching Carl's wrist, Archie fell on his back and straightened the hostage arm between his own legs which pinned his opponent to the mat. This was an "arm bar" and the final step in the technique was to lift his hips off the mat, thus applying pressure on the outstretched arm at the back of the elbow. As Archie lifted his pelvis so, Carl did something rather unexpected. He swung his body on the mat so it was in line with Archie's and his arm was now pointing straight up. In the same motion, he rolled like a crocodile in a death throw, turning Archie on his stomach. In this position, Archie could not apply any pressure to the elbow that was against the mat. In fact, Archie was now in the less than favorable position.

As the two fighters grappled on the floor, each trying to dominate the other, Archie became aware of the other's superior ground game. It seemed he was simultaneously being attacked on three fronts. When moved his left arm to block a choke, he felt his right become captive. At the same time Carl moved past his hips, a vital vanguard in wrestling. It was a though he were being hounded by a three headed guard dog, only this infernal mongrel was not trying to keep him out as much as deny him any escape.

Sensing this danger, he released Carl and regained his feet. The crowd booed as Archie allowed Carl to rise as well, but Archie was cautious now. Something was amiss. Carl's skills were expert, well beyond what Archie had encountered in this club before.

Carl moved in for a take down, eager to scoop Archie off his feet and return him to the mat. Archie parried the move with sharp palm strikes to Carl's stooped shoulders while simultaneously side stepping. This dropped Carl to one knee, annoyed. He rose furtively, back handing Archie in the groin as the bell signaling the end of the round sounded. The dirty blow felt like a bullet in the belly, but Archie only sneered and stood upright, resisting the urge to bend over and puke. As Carl stepped arrogantly past him, Archie gripped the other fighter's shorts and tugged them down to floor.

The crowd broke out into vicious laughter like a pack of jackals as Carl nearly tripped with his shorts around his ankles with only his jock strap for sparse coverage of his ghastly white ass. He tried to come back at Archie, but was intercepted by his trainer and corner man who yanked him to him away.

Archie eased onto the waiting stool in his corner, returning Carl's seething glare with an amused smile. He gave Carl a provoking wink before tilting his head back to receive the water Mackey poured down his throat while methodically inspecting Archie's face for injury.

"You gotta protect that eye, Arch," Mackey advised as he retrieved an eye iron from his bucket of ice and pressed the curved piece of freezing metal to the swelling skin under Archie's left eye which inflammation was already starting to purse close. Archie peered out of his other eye, seeking Byron. He spotted him near the cage door, whispering with a hoodlum.

A ring girl in only bra and panties sashayed into the cage with a number two placard carried over her head as the announcer said, "Let's hear it for the lovely, the sexy, Vanessa! Gentlemen, if this view isn't enough, you can see her live this weekend at Fantasies on Fifth. Be sure to make it rain! I think she should just change her name to Viagra...Oh man, she's making my pants tight!"

As she sashayed by, Archie made a point to brush Mackey aside and fall at her feet as she passed, praising her as though she were a goddess.

Outside the cage, Byron passed the hoodlum a wad of cash before stepping onto the mat to press the showboating Archie back into his stool.

He clasped Archie by the shoulder and said, "All right, brother. I think we have to change our strategy."

"You think?" Archie retorted as he spit blood into the tin bucket between his legs. The fight was not going well and he wasn't happy about it.

"I just found out this guy was the North Carolina three time wrestling champ."

Archie chuckled sardonically. "Got any more jokes?"

"I'm sorry brother. I didn't know," Byron confessed bitterly, guilt tensing his voice.

Archie immediately regretted his own tone. This wasn't Byron's fault. In fact, this was exactly why Byron had opposed fighting here in the first place. Nobody revealed their true fight experience which made fair match ups impossible.

"Nah, not your fault man, I'm sure he didn't

advertise it. Good on you for finding out at all," Archie said apologetically.

Bryon recognized his fighter was trying to console him, even though it was Archie's ass on the line. He was touched, but he didn't like it, not here in the corner. He wanted Archie's mind on intentional violence. He handled Archie roughly by the shoulders and looked sternly him in the eyes. "Look, Arch, he's in Heaven down there on that mat. That's exactly where he wants to be. It's stand up time. Throw some heavy leather, brother. Go to blows and tear into him!"

Archie nodded grimly as a crowd member passed his mouth piece through the cage to Mackey who slapped it into Archie's mouth. He immediately spit it out and called over his shoulder, "Yuck! Who's drinking gin?"

Archie stood as Mackey yanked the stool out from under him and walked towards the center of the ring, holding his mouthpiece and running his tongue over his teeth, mumbling to himself, "I fuckin' hate gin."

Carl responded from across the cage as his corner men ran meticulous last minute checks on him. "I'll smack the taste out of your mouth in a minute."

Archie tapped a pretend watch on his wrist. "Well, chop chop, Princess. I haven't got all night. You didn't chip a nail on my brass balls did you?"

Carl pushed his corner men aside and tossed his stool out of the cage door in a not so subtle hint that he was ready to fight. When the entourage had cleared the cage, the doors were latched and the bell sounded. Archie hardly moved as Carl approached in haste. When Carl appeared in range, Archie let loose two rapid fists. A light left jab to find that Carl's head was in striking distance and a follow up, power right cross to Carl's chin. Only Carl's chin wasn't there when the fist arrived. He had bobbed his head to avoid the cross, but Archie followed through, connecting with a loud thud into Carl's shoulder.

Carl spun on his heel, turning away from Archie and clutching his shoulder in pain, clearly hurt. Archie gave Carl a theatrical and dismissive kick to his ass as the referee seized his arm and raised it to the ceiling in victory. The cage doors were thrust open, corner men and trainers rushing the mat.

As Carl was being helped out of the cage, Archie overheard him tell his trainer, "He dislocated my shoulder…Yeah, with a fuck'n punch!"

CHAPTER TWO

Back in the empty locker room, Archie pulled

his jeans up to his waist and ran the leather belt through

the custom silver and gold buckle. A few years earlier,

Byron had given it as a congratulatory gift when Archie

had won another club's title belt. Of course, the trophy

belt was too large and gaudy to be worn casually, so this

buckle was a scaled down version of that belt with,

"T-N-T engraved in raised lettering.

After slipping a white t-shirt on, Archie glanced to

the door way to find Joe leaning against the jam.

AGAMEMNON

Joe bore his thick, hairy arms folded across his

chest, evidence that he still hit the gym even as he

entered his sixtieth year, but they rested on the oddly

firm potbelly which betrayed him as a man inclined to

fulfilling his indulgences. The cheap bulb in the light

above bounced off a forehead made excessively long by

a retreating hairline. He picked at a canine with a toothpick before sucking his teeth and speaking with a Yankee accent often incomprehensible to the Southern drawls of North Carolina. "I think you decommissioned The Machine. Nearly unhinged his shoulder anyways. I hear he's at the ER getting cortisone pumped into it."

Archie shook his head as he began to unwrap one of his fists. "That's too bad. I'm always in it to win it, but I didn't really mean to hurt him. Well, not permanently anyways."

Joe stepped from the doorway, pulling his toothpick from his mouth and leveling it at Archie. "Don't give me that shit. I don't know what Byron is teaching you guys but I don't want fighters getting hurt like that. This is a sport! Entertainment, got it? This is not the fucking Colosseum. It's a night club." Then, poking his own chest for emphasis, he added, "*My* night club."

Archie recoiled from the statement as though the

words were so ridiculous it was offensive. "Oh please. Don't give me THAT shit. If you were really concerned about fighters getting hurt you wouldn't let Heckman fight here."

"What's that supposed to mean?" Joe asked, feigning puzzlement.

"Like you don't know? He's a professional fighter, Joe. At least he was," Archie said, gesturing toward the bloody mop head which was propped up in the corner behind him before continuing. "The UFC nailed him last year for steroids. Now he's riding out his suspension down here on twice the juice, breaking the faces of a bunch of amateurs... How much does his manager pay for the flesh punching bags?"

Joe waved a dismissive paw. "Hey Junior, I'm trying to run a business here, all right? I don't need to take morality lessons from some kid who just got done sucking his mother's tit. What are you 25, 26?"

Archie winced, not at the words but at the sharp, shooting pain boring into the back of his eyes. He wanted to rub his eyes but one socket was already bruised, so he massaged his temples in an attempt to assuage the increasingly frequent migraine into submission. He took a bottle of aspirin from his bag as he spoke. "I'll have you know, I'm 27 and three quarters, you geriatric fuck. Though, I can understand you being baffled; I've become twice the man you are in half the time."

"If you are such a man, why don't you fight Heckman? Huh?" Joe countered.

"Me? Nah. Not now, and not ever. I'm nobody's fool, Joe. Least of all yours. I fight fair fights. That wouldn't be a fair fight. No one here can give Heckman that while he's on the roids and he loves it. And this ain't baseball where all that means is he'll hit a few more balls out of the park. This is fighting for fuck's sake. The extra dose is to break bones and faces. I only feel bad for the up and comers who are trying to get a start and don't know any better."

"Come on, Arch. You and him, it'll be the biggest fight I've had yet in this joint," Joe goaded as Archie gulped down a handful of aspirin. This was Joe's true motive and weekly ritual, trying to goad and guile Archie into a match against Heckman. True, one look at Heckman was enough to discern his continued use of anabolic steroids, but his previous professional fame made him the club's biggest attraction…next to Archie, who earned it by his cocky showmanship. Joe had sensed for some time a growing disinterest in Heckman's fights. He tore through his opponents with ease, never truly challenged. It only made sense now to pit him against Archie, the other crowd favorite.

His nightclub was a dive and the fights were the only thing bringing in the money, but Joe needed to keep the act exciting like a Ringling Brother's circus. Only Archie was proving to be no dancing bear.

Archie ran his fingers through his hair and moved toward the door, pausing to look Joe in the eye as he lectured, "You mentioned the Colosseum before, Joe...well, you should know, it was built for entertainment, and back then that meant killing Christians for the amusement of a race of doomed Romans. That isn't going to happen here."

To stand both of these men before the same ruins would have yielded very different sentiments. Joe would have felt his forefathers' legacy as a pressure to build upon their mortar. Archie, a past already possessed by others. They had their turn. Now was his time. It was the subject of tomorrow on which they found some accord in a growing disappointment that the world was meant to break.

As Archie stepped past him and into the

nightclub hall, Joe took a stack of folded bills with a blue rubber band from his pocket and called, "Hey, Hotshot, don't forget your purse."

He flung it at Archie who spun and caught it easily.

"Unless you crazy Christians like fighting for free?"

Archie slipped it into his jeans as he turned on his heel, "You, I might fight for free one of these days, Joe."

Joe chuckled to himself and hollered after him, "The *cahones* on you. Tell Sidney you got a round on the house, kid!"

When Archie was gone, Joe's smile faded. He took the bloody mop head from the corner and examined it a contemplative moment before away with self-contempt. Archie may have been his junior, but he wielded his words as well as his fists and had struck Joe where it counted.

CHAPTER THREE

Archie was leaning with an elbow on a cocktail table, discussing his "Greek Physique" with two excitable club bunnies. He lifted weights to build his muscles, read books to keep his mind sharp and plied his charm to put both to use. While he enjoyed the effect he had on women, he relished the effect they had on him all the more. They inspired him to witty, clever repertoire and it culminated in a brief version of him that could not exist without the interaction.

He leaned in close to the blonde and said, "Well, let me ask you this: What's your favorite muscle on a guy?"

The ditsy blonde sipped on her drink which had more ingredients than she had relevant thoughts per day and replied, "Hmmm, I like shoulders, yeah, like definitely, for sure."

The brunette, first annoyed by Archie's presence, now seemed oddly bothered about being ignored by him.

Was her friend so much more attractive than her? Why wasn't this guy talking to her? In an overt effort to gain his attention, she chimed in before her friend could say anymore, "What's your favorite muscle on a girl?" Now he could sense she even felt embarrassed by the insecurity which had permeated her tone.

Archie had been waiting for this, deliberately giving her the cold shoulder she would have given him had he sought her attention from the start. He looked at her a moment, as though she was intruding on the conversation, but softened and smiled as though noticing her for the first time, saying, "I'm starting to think it's whatever ones are responsible for your smile."

The brunette flushed at the unexpected come on as Byron approached Archie from behind, draping an arm over him. "The man of the hour. Okay if I steal him away ladies?"

The brunette, now suddenly bashful, smiled

from behind her glass and said, "Only if you bring him back," earning a dirty look from the blonde.

Archie followed Byron to their favorite stools at the corner bar where Byron could keep an eye on the fights while Archie on the entrance and exits.

"Only two girls tonight, Arch?"

Archie shrugged as he hailed the bartender. "Eh, I'm pacing myself."

Byron laughed at the cocky response. "Ok, just making sure you aren't losing that magic touch."

Recognizing Archie and recalling his usual, the bartender slid a Jameson on the rocks across the grimy bar. As the whisky touched his lips, Archie glanced back at the two young women who returned his look with an eager wave.

"Truthfully, girls have been coming to me pretty easily lately. The irony is that I couldn't care less! I mean, a few years ago the attention would have been great, but they were nowhere around. Now, I've just got other priorities."

Bryon nodded the nod of knowing from experience. "You've been training like a monk. A life of discipline. That's why monks are abstinent, you know. God is their priority...But these girls..." Byron motioned at the ladies at the table and others teetering by in short skirts and pumps, "Most of them have this aching hole in their hearts and they are looking to fill it with anything. Booze, nice clothes, compliments from guys... Thing is, that hole can only be fully filled by God. That's what fulfillment really means and that's what they're looking for. They can sense that God is with you and that's what's attracting them to you."

Archie nodded, surveying the club's feminine clientele, noting a median age among them of twenty-one at most. This was still four years shy of when the human brain reached full maturity. Past that final stage of development, most women came to places like this far less often and were much more wary when they did. Finally, he quipped, "Well, I think I've been, "fulfilling" the wrong hole. I mean, as a sporting man, I admit I enjoy the flirting...but I can't be with them all."

"Try picking just one. What about Meaghan? That girl is a keeper, man. Big breasts and she's crazy about you."

"Yeah, we have plenty in common. We both think I'm great. And she's definitely wife material. I'm just not sure that I'm husband material anymore and that's what she's gonna want one day."

Byron looked at Archie sideways, knowingly. "I know you're still torn up about what happened to Diane, Arch. Probably always will be. But she'd want you to be happy."

Diane. The name was a dagger to his heart, such that he could not speak it and breathe after without pain.

Instead, he wore her name stamped into the steel KIA bracelet on his wrist. He used to carry her picture in his wallet, but he had stopped upon noticing that she seemed to be getting younger and younger in the photo, appearing less like a woman and more like a girl. Of course, the photo couldn't be changing. Instead, Archie knew that he was the one who was changing, getting older while she had long ceased to live. So Archie didn't answer Byron, but emptied his glass at the thought and waved it at the bartender for a refill. Taking notice, Byron said, "I won't say anything because it's fight night, but lay off that piss. It's no good for anyone and even worse for a fighter."

Happy to talk about anything but Diane, Archie retorted, "That's not, not saying anything. And I don't think God has anything against drinking. Oh, you laugh, but Jesus turned water into wine, Byron! He could have turned it into antibiotics or gold coins, but he turned it to wine."

"He did a lot of stuff like that, Arch. That's how God shows Himself. By making the impossible, possible."

Archie held his fresh beverage high in the air, admiring it as he spoke. "I think that alcohol is a holy substance."

Byron answered by laughing at the proposed apotheosis.

"Think about it. When you drink, you start to lose your body. It goes numb, you lose coordination and control over it. Even your vision doesn't work right."

"Exactly, why is that a good thing?

"Because at the same time, your spirit swells. You feel happy and you feel good. You become more spirit than body! Hell, we have all seen that drunk guy going around telling everyone he loves them. Jesus said love thy neighbor, didn't He?

"I'm still not buying it. That alcohol is somehow a holy gift from God."

"If we are all just souls trapped in human bodies, is it so far-fetched to think God would give us a gift, a thing to let us have some relief from said body?"

"Maybe you're on to something. Maybe, but what you have to think about is moderation. Food is good for you, but you eat too much and you will die a glutton. Sleep too much and you are a sloth. You need balance. Nobody got drunk at the last supper."

"So Ying and Yang, huh, Mr. Miyagi?"

"Ying and Yang, Daniel-San."

Byron and Archie shifted in their stools to give their attention to the octagon which the better half of the patrons were now rushing towards in excitement as another fighter entered the cage.

HECTOR

Heckman stalked the perimeter of the cage as

the stage lights glistened off the twitching and vacillating striations of his muscle-bound body. His back, shoulders and traps were disproportionately large to his frame, giving him an aesthetically appealing V-shape which tapered into a slim waist. Most only looked in admiration and awe at this Adonis flesh, not recognizing it as the gift of the steroids which were extra potent on those muscles that contained the most receptors for the drug. Upon that broad back was a portrait of a sheet clad ghost with the word, "BOO!" stamped above it. Stopping in his tracks like a wolf catching the scent of nearby prey, Heckman turned towards the bar, locking his eyes on Archie.

"Somebody seems to like you," Byron said.

Archie shrugged it off. "Eh, when you're popular."

"He's a good fighter, Arch. You gotta give him that."

"Everyone is a good fighter on steroids, Byron," Archie replied. As far as he was concerned, Heckman had made a deal with the devil. He would have his victories now, but they would be superficial. And one day it would be over and he would have nothing else, not even his health. His liver would fall out and then his kidneys would burst and his heart would clog up tight. And make no mistake - that will be the devil cashing in. Few things were as important to Archie as his bodily health. The thought of being handicapped in any way, terrified him as a severe limitation on his autonomy, his very freedom. Archie frowned at the very thought and slid some cash across the bar to saddle up.

"You're not even going to watch him fight?" Byron asked in surprise.

Archie shook his head and then winced at the ensuing pang the movement caused him. He grabbed his temples and said, "It won't be a fight. It will be another rook getting a straight beating. Haven't got the stomach for it. Besides, I gotta nurse this headache."

"I don't know. I heard this story once, David and Goliath. I think one day, someone with more faith than Heckman has juice is gonna take him outta here for good."

Archie only said, "I'll see you in the morning, bro," as he gave Byron an embrace.

"All right, love ya, brother. Good fight tonight."

"I learn from the best. Love you, man," Archie replied before departing.

He felt Heckman's gaze boring into him as he made his way through the crowd and close to the cage but didn't return it in any capacity. Bryon watched this curiously from his stool. When Archie was gone from sight, Heckman fixed his gaze on Bryon and added a sadistic smirk. As the ring girl passed Heckman, he grabbed her ass with a forceful snare. She yelped in pain and whirled around, slapping him across his face. His smile instantly dropped as he seized her hand in anger, drawing her close. His cornermen rushed to intervene, one escorting her from the cage while the other whispered in Heckman's ear as though taming a wild horse. Pacified into his corner, Heckman returned his vicious eyes to Bryon, spitting on the mat to show his contempt for everything.

CHAPTER FOUR

Archie slowed his black motorcycle to a stop before the red light, the nearby street lamp reflecting off the lightening decals on the gas tank where, "Greece Lightening" was painted in electric blue. His helmet hung off the back rest, something he would don only if stopped by an officer of the law. Archie knew it was dangerous to ride without it, but he held the same attitude toward condoms. Both were probably a good idea, but then the ride just didn't feel the same. Besides, it reminded him of the staggering weight and stifling strap of the Kevlar helmet that he once wore as a commandeered horse bares bridle and bit in bondage.

He looked longingly at the rusted 1969 Mustang Boss which was parked on a lawn with, "For Sale" spray painted on its faded white side. The light turned green, but there was no traffic behind him, so he lingered to adore the car a moment more. Archie had an affinity for all modes of transportation, which he saw as extensions of his freedom. The more of them he owned, the freer he felt. The carcass of a car wasn't priced too far beyond his reach, but the added cost of body work was. *One day though*, he consoled himself before rolling back on the throttle an instant before the light turned back to red.

The wind in his face turned pleasantly salty, the ocean odor signaling he was almost home. He did a double take as he glided into the marina, recognizing a familiar vehicle in the otherwise empty lot. He parked the motorcycle by the four tiered boat rack stacked with assorted small speedboats and walked to the old sedan to peer into the driver's side window. He smiled at the small form and blonde hair dozing in the reclined driver's seat.

BRISEIS

Meaghan responded to his gentle knock on the glass by waking from her slumber and rubbing the sleep out of her make up covered eyes. Even though it was close to three in the morning, she had not been asleep very long. Her shift at the strip club had ended less than an hour ago and though she was tired and Archie's place was farther than her own, she had made the trip.

She had been a dancer for well over a year, and for the most part, she was confident enough about herself not to worry about the social stigma. Not that she didn't find some veracity in that view either. It was a seedy business and many of the girls danced to drown their troubles and traumas in booze and drugs, though Meaghan contended that these girls were toxic to themselves long before they became exotic entertainers. No, she was determined to defy the cliché by keeping a level head and actually using the revenue to complete her college education.

All the same dancing took a toll, for while it may have seemed like a choice, the pressure to succeed as a professional woman was a sort of bondage. She could face her slavery now, or pretend it didn't exist until it was before her as a tremendous mountain of debt.

In a way, her studies into psychology bolstered her mentally, making her more capable of separating her dancing from her self-image. Still, there were some nights even she had her doubts. Some customers debasement hit a mark and she needed to be reminded that she was not just sexy, but beautiful and the way Archie looked at her was enough.

They had met the first night Meaghan was assigned to the Rock's nightclub as a ring girl and server. She was delivering water to the makeshift locker room, when she first saw him staring pensively at the wall through a thousand yard stare. The other fighters responded to her in a way that would have made construction workers blush, but he hadn't even noticed her. He was fixed, unmoving and uninterested in anything around him. That all changed when he got in the cage. He came alive and couldn't hide his passion. Meaghan had heard it took a lot of heart to fight, but she came to an observant understanding, that some fighters fought better with a broken heart.

She herself had the fight of her life that same night when two drunks dragged her into a supply closet. They tore at her skimpy outfit and didn't even bother to cover her mouth as her desperate screams would never be heard over the thunderous club music. And then suddenly, they were the ones screaming as Archie ripped them out of the closet and pummeled them with a metal napkin dispenser. As they bled on the floor, he took one of the few remaining napkins from the smashed dispenser and pressed it to her tear stained cheeks as he helped her from the closet.

They had been seeing each other ever since but Archie was as diligent to remind her that they were not, "an item" as she was careful not to press it. That was the response she had gotten from him when she offered to stop dancing. While he contended it was none of his business, he did ask for a small concession. His request was she never take the shift at the Rock's again. At least the strip club was upscale, as far as such places ever were, and more importantly, they had professional security on hand for the dancers. The Rock's on the other hand, had been closed five times in as many years because of stabbings, drug and prostitution charges and even a brawl where someone was killed. All in all, it was an easy agreement to make and Meaghan had the looks to make the refusal to her boss.

Archie shook his head and tapped his watch with pretend impatience as Meaghan labored to crank down the window on the outmoded car, a matter for which Archie frequently teased her. The vehicle was old, but it was hers and deep down she knew her well-being was at the heart of Archie's jabs, hoping to inspire her towards

a ride with modern safety features.

"Hey, Soldier. How'd it go?" she greeted.

"I'm still the champ, Bombshell. What are you

doing here?"

"I guess I just missed you. Work was…"

Meaghan just sighed instead of finishing the sentence.

As she stepped out of the car, she continued, "I just can't

wait to graduate and be a psychologist already.

Hopefully I don't lose my own mind first. I thought

you'd be happy to see me. I can go..."

"Nah, I am. I'll just be happier to see you when

you're naked," Archie said, taking her and kissing her.

While most men were happy to see her naked and paid

for the privilege, the comment was still a sincere flattery

to Meaghan since Archie hadn't taken the impromptu

visit as a chance to set boundaries between them,

confirming the meaning of their relationship that was

supposedly not a relationship.

As Meaghan pulled away from the kiss, she looked into Archie's eyes and noticed the bruise deepening his right socket. "You know, when I said blue went well with your eyes, this isn't what I meant."

Archie laughed. "I know, but this guy threw punches like a jack in the box. Just, pow! Outta nowhere."

As they strolled under the stilted boathouse and to the ramp which jutted over the water, Meaghan slipped her arm around Archie's and leaned her head on his shoulder. He rapped his knuckles against the worn wooden rail as they walked, a deliberate habit he adopted to calcify the joints he wielded daily as weapons.

"Why do you do it, Archie? The fighting, I mean."

"I heard this German word once, sounded like,

funktionslust, but I remember it as function lust. Basically, lusting for whatever it is you do well. Whatever your function is. I'm a fighter because I'm good at it. It's my function."

"Yeah, love what you do, I get it. But fighting is such a brutal sport. You can't enjoy that."

Archie reflected as he stretched a sore arm behind him. It was indeed a brutal sport. He was beat up even when he won.,

"Truthfully, I hardly ever remember the actual fight. It's just a flash. It's all the training that comes before the fight. That's the real competition and all athletes love that. The only real difference in fighting and any other sport comes after the fight. When you're standing alone. Winning a fight, Meg...it's like nothing else. You're standing there, and you know you could have lost and you're just so grateful you didn't. It's like life after a near death experience, every time."

They were near the end of the ramp now, pausing to look out over the dark waters at the distant flashing of yellowish lightening that erupted silently over the North Carolina coast. Meaghan didn't say anything, nor did she want to. With another man, she would have felt compelled to comment on the beautiful scene, to point out the obvious that it was in fact, beautiful. By now she had become accustomed to these moments at Archie's side. She used to wonder what he was contemplating at these times, but gradually she learned for herself. It was an opportunity to just be and observe; a chance to stop contemplating. For all his wisecracks and sarcasm, there was a serious complexity to Archie. He had a big persona, one that often completely masked his true being. Maybe it was her endeavors in the field of psychiatry that made her more perceptive than most and able to see the real him, but she couldn't help feeling it was more than that…that it was love and a two way love at that. A love he didn't condone in words but permitted by sharing these moments with her.

At last, the juncture passed and they took another shorter ramp to a floating dock at the end of the which floated Archie's vessel and home, an old thirty foot sailboat that was in a constant state of do it yourself repairs. The sight of the boat always made Archie nostalgic, remembering the first time he laid eyes on her only a few years ago. After separating from the Army, he spent the bulk of his deployment money on his motorcycle and set out on the road for three months. He wandered the country he had fought for, searching for something that had made it worth it. He ended in North Carolina simply because that was where the gas money had run out.

The economic recession was in full bloom and veterans, even decorated ones like Archie, weren't getting hired. It didn't help that he had never planned for a time after the Army, not for a lack of foresight as much as surprise to find he was to be living at all. Every day of war demanded his immediate attention if he were to survive it, such that he could spare no consideration for a tomorrow that was never guaranteed to arrive.

The vintage sloop was in such poor shape and priced so low, he was able to buy it with his first unemployment check if he didn't eat. The previous owner had abandoned her in a small cove, which suited Archie as he could afford no rent and would live off the land - or water in this case. He recalled the day he fell in love with her as he rowed to her ignoble ruins, realizing that they were both in poor condition and yet were serving to keep the other afloat.

With the money from his fights, he was eventually able to move her to this marina which facilitated his ongoing repair work. One of the first things he had done after painting her topside, was to christen her, "Argo" as was now emblazoned on her transom.

Hearing their footsteps on the dock, "Olive" a black and white pointer retriever, emerged from the makeshift doggy door that had been fitted into the hatchway. She ran to the bow to whine and wag her tail until Archie was close enough to reach over the water to pet her. He had rescued her from the streets when she was only likely days away from starvation, her puppy ribs pressing through her fur. He nearly died swerving his motorcycle when she darted onto the road before him. When an old woman saw that he had managed to coax the scrappy stray into his arms she admonished him, warning him in broken English that the dog was diseased and dirty. She became exasperated when Archie shrugged her off, thinking he did not understand until he corrected her in her own tongue, "I understand...I just don't care." Having witnessed the extent of human filthiness, even the dirtiest of animals seemed pure to him.

Now she raced nimbly across the deck and disappeared inside the boat as Archie went around to step on the transom. As he did, she emerged again, gingerly carrying a bottle of beer between her teeth.

Meaghan laughed, "You know you have a drinking problem when your dog brings you beer."

"Nah, she just wants me to open it."

Archie lifted his shirt slightly to use the inside of his TNT buckle to pop the cap off the beer, pouring half of it into a dog dish on the deck. Meaghan stared curiously at the buckle as Archie finished the remainder.

"Why do you go by, TNT, Archie?" she asked.

Archie avoided the question by looking at the sky and water as though distracted by the weather. "I think it's going to get a little windy tonight."

"Oh, come on, tell me," Meaghan insisted.

Archie bent over on the deck to untie a line from the boat cleat. "I should probably put a spring line on to keep her from rocking too bad."

Meaghan persisted in a goading voice, "Come on, TNT, you can tell me."

Archie let out a frustrated chuckle of reluctance as he tied a knot in the line. "It's for my mom."

Meaghan wasn't expecting that. She knew Archie's mother had died when he was young from breast cancer, but couldn't fathom a connection to the ring name. "Your mom? TNT?"

"I was 11, maybe 12, when I got it in my head I wanted to be a boxer."

"Imagine that."

"Right? We didn't have money to keep the lights on, but somehow she paid for those lessons. I was just a kid, so I never asked how."

Archie worked with the dock lines as he talked, tying and untying the line around various cleats. "One day, this kid in my class came teasing me, telling me his dad saw my mom dancing at some strip club. He even brought in a newspaper ad. It said something about featuring TNT at the local club."

"Oh my...what did you say?"

Archie shrugged with the lines in his hands. "Nothing, but I got my first knockout. I knew he was telling the truth though. I had seen her write TNT on some of her CD's."

"Did you say anything to her?"

Archie finished with the line and pushed the hatch to the boat open. He flipped the breaker and the lights came on in the cabin. "Nah. She must have been ashamed if she never told me. But that was the worst part! That she was doing this for me and yet she was shamed by it. Shame is the worst thing a person can feel, because then they start thinking they aren't worth God's attention when nothing could be farther from the truth."

Meaghan quickly tried to recall what her textbooks had said about, "Oedipus Complexes." Did that apply here? She was a stripper, just like his mother, and he was Greek after all. Then she looked up from her place on the dock, to see Archie offering her his hand to board the Argo. The distance between dock and boat was brief, but Archie's gentleness in the moment answered the question for her. After another night of men possessing her body with their eyes and laps, she now knew why Archie was different. Why he was able to see her as a real person even despite her nightly profession. No, Archie didn't have a maternal imprint for strippers, but the inherent contempt most men felt for dancers was foreign to him.

She accepted his hand as she stepped onto the Argo, saying, "That's beautiful, Archie. She wasn't just trying to feed you, I mean by putting food on the table,

but she was trying to feed your dreams with those

lessons. Honestly, I used to think those ring names you

guys have were a little dumb, but not anymore."

CHAPTER FIVE

Archie cooked on a single burner stove top while Meaghan searched the radio, finally settling on the 50's oldies station she knew Archie favored. Like her, he had to contend with violent, blaring music all night and there was something soothing about these golden aged tunes.

Archie motioned for her to sit at the tiny table only big enough for two as he scooped the steaming contents of the pot into three bowls. He placed one entrée on the deck for Olive and set two more on the table for them. Meaghan peered into his bowl as he sat. "Archie! That's not enough for you. And you gave me more!"

"Oh jeez, they're the same!" Archie said as he shielded his bowl from Meaghan's attempt to parcel her portion into it.

She pushed her meal away and crossed her arms in an overt display of pouting. "I can't eat if I think you're hungry."

Archie just smiled and motioned with his fork for her to dig in. Aware he wouldn't be so easily swayed by feminine wiles, Meaghan reluctantly began to eat.

"I was in Afghanistan, this outpost called Siah Choy. Our cook there was real low on rations. We could tell because he was serving weird combinations like marinara sauce and waffles."

"Oh, gross."

"Oh it was, but thing is, no one complained. Not one person. There's just something real humbling about sharing a meal together when the food is scarce. When you serve yourself, you take less than you want so that there's more for the guy next to you. You watch and he does the same. Everyone puts everyone before themselves. It makes brothers out of men."

Meaghan nodded in understanding. "You know, before I started dancing, I used to wait tables, and believe it or not, the way people treated me was even worse than at the club. I mean, if their food wasn't done fast enough or wasn't absolutely perfect...It's like they'd forget I'm a human being! Yes, I serve you food, but I'm not subservient. And that's why I think gluttony is a sin. I mean, I know that God doesn't hate fat people, so I have to think that putting food over others, even yourself, is what is so wrong."

Archie studied Meaghan for a moment with both admiration and mild surprise. "You know you're pretty wise for such a young girl."

"Oh my...you're barely three years older, Arch."

"That's a big difference! I must be like an old man to you."

"Oh, yeah, you're ancient."

"I'm serious! I don't know how to court a younger woman. I mean, should I take you to the ball pit at McDonald's? Would that be fun for you?"

"Well, did you inherit any stripper moves? Because that would be awesome."

"Please, I put the pole in pole dancing. Check this out."

Archie rose, taking Meaghan's bowl from her. Reaching overhead, he flicked the light to its red bulb, a device intended to preserve a sailors natural night vision but he was using facetiously to set the mood. He leaned over her, whispering against her neck. "The real trick, when giving women a lap dance, is to give them exactly what they want."

"Yeah? And what do women want?"

"Let me show you," Archie said, guiding Meaghan's hand to his back pocket, "Yeah, you like feeling that big...hard...wallet, don't you?"

"You're ridiculous," Meaghan laughed.

"With an emphasis on the dick," Archie countered, "And don't you dare pardon that pun."

Meaghan giggled and squirmed playfully as Archie tried to kiss her. "Are you going to show me the captain's log now?"

"As a matter of fact, I was just thinking I might make an entry."

Meaghan burst into laughter which Archie stifled with a consuming kiss.

CHAPTER SIX

It was the middle of the night at a small outpost in Afghanistan. Archie crept through the camp, his camouflage uniform concealing him even deeper in the darkness. He knelt before a makeshift animal trap some of his platoon members had made out of concertina wire and parachute cord. Carefully, he removed a slab of SPAM meat from the snare.

They had been waking up to find large cat footprints around their tents. Huge. It spooked the men and this trap was one of their many attempts to catch it. Not knowing Archie's routine of sabotaging the trap, this mysterious feline had grown to mythological proportions in their minds as a kind of giant apex predator with super intelligence.

A voice broke the night, startling him.

PENTHESILEA

"Doesn't that defeat the point?" Diane said as Archie turned to face her. She was in her very early 20's, with a flawless snow white complexion that contrasted starkly against the camouflage pattern of her uniform. She had a nurturing face that made redundant the red cross patch of a medic on her shoulder.

"There's some kind of animal scoping out the camp at night. Got the guys scared and they want to catch it.

"I heard something about that. You don't think it's just some fat, stray Afghani cat?"

"Saw it myself, coming down from the tower the other night. It was like part tiger, part wolf, if that makes any sense. I've been around GI's enough to know they will kill it if they can," Archie said. He knew his fellow soldiers were good men, but like most people, they feared the unknown and sought to destroy it. In a war zone, where humans were killing each other was the daily imperative, their cruelty towards the animal would be permissive and without restraint.

"But you're a G.I." Diane pointed out.

"I'm not that kind of G.I." was his reply.

And then he was there, wounded in a medical tent with Diane checking his bandage. She smiled at him and then -

Archie was in his Army dress uniform and Diane in her Naval dress uniform, looking splendid together at a military ball. Archie was on one knee, proposing with a ring in his hand when -

He was in Iraq, in the passenger seat of an MRAP, pounding the steel dashboard with his hand, watching the smoke rise from the tent he and Diane secreted away to on occasion as it was hardly used. He had asked her to wait for him there, but his convoy mission had taken longer than expected and he was late. Just as he was entering the base, there was a mortar attack. Diane worked in the hospital, the only hardened facility on base and the safest place to be during an indirect fire attack. If not for him, she would have been there. She would have been safe.

Archie leaped out of the MRAP before it even stopped, running into the smoking ruins of the large military tent. He emerged carrying Diane. She was dead and it was his fault. He dropped to his knees, tilting his head back and screaming.

Archie woke suddenly and violently, finishing his scream and startling Meaghan awake. His eyes darted around the dark cabin as though he were unsure of his surroundings. Meaghan touched him softly on the arm, reassuring him of his location. "Archie! It's ok, it's ok.

It's over, it was just a dream."

"No. It wasn't," Archie said, disgusted with himself and the cold sweat that covered him. The first time he woke to a cold sweat was after he had come back from Iraq. He had thought then that the extreme heat of the desert had triggered his body to sweat profusely and it would simply take it time to readjust to a temperate climate. It wasn't until later he learned it was a symptom of Post-Traumatic Stress and its reoccurrence tonight demonstrated he was not nearly as recovered as he had thought himself to be.

"Iraq or Afghanistan this time?" Meaghan cooed gently in the dark.

"Both," Archie replied harshly. He cringed at hearing his own rough voice resound in the peaceful night. It was a familiar tone, curt and hard but not the one he had intended to use. It belonged to another, a former self. Only a moment before he had been the part of him he was supposed to leave behind…the well trained savage. Deadly, dangerous and perfectly suited to the environment of war. The transformation from man to beast was as easy as closing his eyes, but returning to civility was never part of his training. He plied his thick lips into a soft smile and kissed Meaghan awkwardly as a dragon might try to caress its captive maiden while lacking any gentle accouterments…only scales, teeth and claws.

"Where are you going?" Meaghan asked as he pulled the covers over her. Coaxing his baritone into a soft whisper he said, "You get your beauty sleep. You have a lot to maintain."

She rolled over on her stomach and watched as he pushed back the hatch and slipped topside with sneakers in hand. As an attractive young woman, she thought she knew what it was to be objectified. As a stripper with a brain, she capitalized on it. That eighty-five million years of evolution led to her getting the precise combination of DNA to make her most appealing to the most amount of men, was the ultimate goal of the process. How many billions suffered natural selection, born with useless flippers, spina bifida and eating disorders to achieve the perfection in the physical form she possessed? Despite the instances of sexism, she knew she was lucky. In general, men admired respectfully, and she wasn't going to hold them all accountable for the exceptions of the few.

As Archie closed the hatch behind him, it hurt her to know, that while being a sex object had it perks, being soldier had none. She felt Archie had so much to offer, but something, war most likely, kept him unable from delivering. The man could not even sleep, much less devote himself to another profession or commit to another person. He had experienced the true objectification men had known throughout all of history. He had been rendered a brute tool for feeble politicians, little more than a shield or appendage affixed to a trigger. Without war, he might have been capable of anything. He might even have been able to love her.

***

Archie sat on the deck of the Argo as the sun bloomed over the watery horizon, loosening his laces after he over tightened them in his agitation. It was at times like this he had to remind himself to bury the animal. Meaghan was far from naïve, but how could she understand? Would he even want her to? Iraq and Afghanistan were just distant countries to most people in the same way the moon was only a nearby satellite far removed from their day. Yet for the few astronauts ever to mar that surface, the ghastly orb remained far more tangible in their minds even after their return. Likewise, Archie had made touchdown only to return home to a gravity heavier than he had known before, as though he now carried the combined weight of the land where he was and had been simultaneously.

As a boy, he knew a veteran or two who refused to talk about their war experiences. It had always baffled Archie, but now he understood the futility of trying to explain what could only be experienced. As a soldier, he had seen things didn't fit a common frame of reference which isolated him from the better part of humanity. In an effort to understand the world, men examined it near and far through microscopes and telescopes, but to live through war was to forever view life through a kaleidoscope, incomprehensible and twisted distortions of pain and pride, tragedy and triumph, beauty and brutality.

Like the astronaut, entering a warzone for the first time felt like stepping onto another planet where the rules of everything changed. One had to walk with great care or leave the surface forever. A loud noise back home meant a car had back fired or a garbage truck was shaking a dumpster, but on a battlefield it meant someone was probably dying. He recalled watching the helicopter he had just debarked lifting off, spraying his helmet with sand as its blinking lights disappeared into the night sky. His eighteen year old mind came to the quick realization that he was stranded in hell on Earth and that chopper was his only way out. He could no longer go AWOL and run away back to New York. Everyone here wanted him dead. The only way he would see that home again was to fight his way out of that place. That was why he fought at first, for his own self-preservation. It demanded he become a savage, and hate became a necessary component to that end. When hatred has free reign, it quickly becomes all-consuming and with time and personal loss, Archie became a man who lived to kill.

He adopted the natural "us versus them" mentality in regards to the enemy, aware that deep in his mind, the former possessed an elevated height over the latter. The "us" were good men and decent humans while the "them" were something less…and cruelty to something less than human is far too easy. The enemy thought the same way, albeit it in their terms. To them, he was an, "infidel" and there was no such thing as a sin against a non-believer, no torture they could not exact on his flesh if they were ever to seize it.

There was the day Archie held the enemy through his rifle scope, his finger aching longingly on the trigger and his mouth watering in anticipation. As he swallowed the bitter saliva, he recognized it as hate manifested in his physical being. The foul sentiment now had a taste which he knew and could never wash from his mouth.

Most things were difficult to see when occurring

in miniature, subtle amounts like a speck of dirt on a blank canvas but his acquaintance with hate was a bucket of mud splattered on a white wall. Hate appeared to him with the clarity that accompanies such intense abundance. He saw it clearly and recognized it for what it was...evil. Since then, he made an effort to purge his being of that soul scouring poison, but he knew there were others who embraced it. Most were blind to it, encouraged by parents since childhood that there is nothing hiding under the bed. Having come face to face with such evil, Archie knew full well that it existed in this world which he would never sleep soundly in again.

Removing his steel KIA bracelet and placing it near the helm, he skillfully dressed his hands in black boxing wraps. He finished preparing his fists as he dismounted his vessel to make his way toward the boat house by way of the wooden ramp which was slippery with morning dew. The weather-beaten structure was elevated on stilts to prevent it from being washed away by the rising waters of the rare but inevitable hurricane. Underneath the boathouse was a decked area which housed the dock master's small office and was a comfortable place for boat owners to hide from the midday heat. An out dated Coca-Cola machine hummed loudly next to an ice box behind which Archie retrieved a green Army duffel bag, heavy as he had filled it with beach sand years before. Using a wooden bench as a stepping stool, he attached the duffel to a hook affixed to the overhang.

He shoved the bench aside and began to spar with the bag, slowly at first but with increasing intensity as his muscles and tendons began to loosen up from his tense slumber. He was known as a cage fighter, but that title he had always found lacking as his fight didn't end when the bell rang and he left the cage. He was always fighting. The cage was just the one place victory couldn't run from him, couldn't hide and taunt him. He couldn't face his personal losses head on, not really. The past was unwinnable, but in the cage he could wrestle victory with his own two hands and when his arm was raised in the air, he was a winner and no one could take that from him. He was pummeling the bag now, his shoulders aching from the same effort which burned his lungs. He only ceased when his throat was too parched to swallow. Then he made his way back to the Argo to strip down to his underwear before leaping off the transom, diving deep into the salt laden waters.

The aqua embraced him, almost maternally, as though he were a son returning to the womb, hearing only a gentle swooshing and his own heart beat as he plunged into the dark and murky embrace. Then he let the buoyant water lift him gently to her surface, all the while as she cooled, cuddled and cleansed him. He lived on her waves which nightly rocked him to sleep using the Argo as a bassinet. He awoke only shortly before as an infant in that cradle, crying out, and now the water was here to comfort and nourish her child as a mother's milk. Then he splashed through that water, playfully, as though a gleeful toddler grasping at his mother's face. The water often beckoned and he always answered the summons, no matter what he was doing, like an obedient boy leaving his playmates without so much as a goodbye when his matriarch called him home.

Wrapped in a blanket, Meaghan stepped sleepily onto the Argo's dew covered deck, watching as Archie dragged his weary body onto the long island that separated the marina from the open ocean. She knew Archie kept his body fit, for having been so well acquainted with violence, he was ever preparing for the next encounter. He never felt safe. For a brief, adventurous moment, she thought to surprise him by swimming out there. It was only 200 meters, but that was one thing in a pool and quite another on those ebbing waves. She wasn't that confident in her swimming abilities and was more than a little wary of the sharks that surely hunted below the surface. Only an hour before, she was wrapped in his arms and now, in typical fashion, he had gone to where she could not follow, placing distance between them where there had been a brevity of tender closeness.

CHAPTER SEVEN

Archie could already hear the praise music through the broad church doors as he made his way up the stone steps. It washed over him as he stepped inside and smiled at the now familiar scene of swaying worshipers in pews while the lively band playing in front of the altar. Though it wasn't always a familiar sight.

When they first met, Byron gave him the church address leaving out the part about it being a church, with instructions to meet him there on a Sunday morning. Archie circled the block a dozen times trying to find a house before he realized it was the church he was looking for. He was not on good terms with God at the time. Archie had been an important man in the military, respected and trusted with tremendous responsibility. To be subjected to toil long, fiscally-strapped months of unemployment and job applications filed in vain took a serious toll on an already taxed soul. Most of the tragedies in his life happened rather quickly and there had been no time to appeal to God for intervention. Time was all he had then, and it trudged by slowly under the strain of misery. Praying and calling potential employers was his constant recourse. Eventually, the unanswered call was too much for him to endure. He severed that tether, though the defiance felt meaningless as he was sure he was already abandoned. There were seven billion souls on the planet and Archie was sure they were all better than his, all more deserving of God's time.

So it was that he first entered that steeple with steel refrain, yet he could not deny the feeling of warmth that washed over him as he crossed the threshold. It felt as though he was stepping out of the cold of a long and lonely winter walk.

Still, as a New York native the southern style of praise was like a carnival compared to any church service he had ever been to, which made him feel even more out of place. As the band played, he made inquiries, looking for Byron until someone pointed to the stage. Bryon was up there, looking out of his mind as he ripped into an electric guitar under a giant holy cross. Archie sat and waited through the following sermon until Bryon finally approached him. This had been a test of sorts, for Byron refused to train any fighter who couldn't sit through a church sermon.

Now Archie made his way down the aisle, shaking hands and embracing the attendees who had become like family to him. He never returned to praying in the manner he had before. He no longer felt the need. He no longer felt abandoned.

At the altar Archie took the roll of money Joe had given him the night before and dropped it in the gold offering pot. Byron nodded his hello as he squeezed out a few more guitar licks before following Archie to a seat in the pews as the band dispersed.

Pastor Bob resembled an older, shorter and bearded Elvis with the same jet black hair, southern swagger and powerful voice. The man had an intuition that bordered on the paranormal. Meaghan had met him only once, and from that sole encounter she believed he was some kind of sage. She had accompanied Archie to church and spent the drive there busy in the passenger side mirror trying to beautify her bed head, while Archie insisted she looked her best with hair up in a simple pony tail. Archie hadn't even the chance to give Pastor Bob her name in introduction before he seized her hand and told her what a beautiful forehead she had, "like Sharon Stone" and advised she ought to wear her hair held back in a ponytail.

Now he strutted across the stage, ebullience in his charismatic baritone. "What motivates you? What is your purpose? That's what y'all really want to know, isn't it? That's why you're here. To have me tell you your purpose for being here. I won't though. It doesn't work like that." As he spoke, an Aunt Jemima look alike, still exalted from the praise music paced the pews yelling, "Oh Jesus, oh lord Jesus!" Archie looked sideways at Byron, causing each other to crack up..

In the back row of the church a homeless man was sleeping. A churchgoer moved to wake him, but Pastor Bob threw a theatrical hand in the air to stop him. "Let that man sleep! This is the only place he can, this house of God."

Pastor Bob walked down the aisle toward the back of the church, calmly side stepping Aunt Jemima who was now running the perimeter of the room. Pastor Bob stood over the dozing vagrant as he orated, "When he leaves this church he is pursued by demons. He gets no peace outside of this church, this shelter of the Almighty. The demons won't leave him be. That's why he's exhausted, tired, ragged, and rundown. You may all think I'm a little cuckoo but I see demons. I see them all around, trying to trick us, distract us, and get us to lose focus on our God given purpose. That's how they win."

Pastor Bob didn't even blink as Aunt Jemima, losing steam, but still at it, shuffled past him huffing, "Praise, Jesus…praise Him."

"God put us here for a purpose, and they want to make sure you cannot achieve that purpose. That's why suicide is so bad a sin. When someone takes their own life, they cannot fulfill their part in God's design." A churchgoer tried to intercept Aunt Jemima who was wheezing as though bordering on collapse, but she brushed them off.

"And let me tell you something else about suicide. It's not something that only happens to those who kill themselves all at once, with a gun or poison or whatever else. Some of us, kill ourselves a little at a time and it's just as awful. We hold on to the hurt and anger of the past, and keep it inside like a spiritual cancer for so long that it sometimes becomes a physical cancer."

After a fellowship lunch of fried chicken and corn, Archie was helping deal out boxes of groceries to those in need. He carried a box to an elderly woman's car and waited patiently while she fished her keys from a purse that weighed more than her bony frame. She returned his effort with a weak hug that made Archie feel like a cheap stuffed animal in a capture claw machine.

Then he went to his motorcycle to retrieve a backpack from the back seat before disappearing down a stairwell into the church basement.

The basement had been turned into an MMA training area by the addition of scraps of old carpet and foam duct taped together to form a mat on the concrete floor. Mackey was already there, grappling with Chris. Chris was a scrawny 14 year-old who was too young to fight at the Rock's, but old enough to get hassled on the streets, which he did, so Byron had taken him in.

Archie crossed the mat, stepping over them to plop down on a rusty metal fold-out chair under a large wooden cross from a church play which was propped up in the corner. He watched the two, making mental notes of their individual strengths and weakness to hone and correct when the moment was most instrumental. Today it was just three of them, but during the working week there were more. Guys who wanted to fight but didn't want to train, and as such, few ever stuck around long. It was understood that Archie was the leader of the crew, and it was this duty which fulfilled him. When in the military, Archie was always a leader, even before his rank officially permitted it. Leading his men, who he loved, into the peril of combat was a role he both dreaded and longed for, like a masochist.

Archie removed his button down shirt and

draped it on the back of the chair. Then he took off his dog tags, hanging them from the arm of the cross.

His shoes and pants were next, revealing his fight shorts underneath. He balanced on one foot in the corner of the mat, grasping his other behind his back to stretch. "Come on, Mack. Make a move. Chris is owning you."

Mackey shot Archie an annoyed look but couldn't respond as Chris pressed his attack.

"Oh man. I'm not even going to be able to call you Mackey anymore. I'm going to have to refer to you as Chris's bitch from now on. Yeah, that's your new name."

Mackey took his mouth piece out, hurling it at Archie.

"Chris, your bitch is getting out of hand. Throwing stuff."

Chris laughed and slapped Mackey across the

face, saying, "Hey, behave bitch."

As Archie tilted the green Army canteen back to wash down more than the recommended dose of Advil, he heard the familiar click clack of his trainer making his way down the hall, a sound like horses hooves on concrete.

CHIRON

Comanche for, "Old Man," Soko had spent most of his life growing into his name until he at last personified it. The aged Indian was approaching his seventieth year, but appeared older, a combination of his pure sagacity and feeble legs which forced him to hobble like a four legged beast, always gripping the crutches braced against his forearms in arthritic hands. He wasn't always crippled, in fact, it was only a decade before that he was struck with the onset of distal muscular dystrophy. Before that, he was a lithe and sturdy man who had earned the nickname "Man O' War" for his four tours in the deep jungles of Viet Nam as a Marine grunt-all voluntary. He was a special asset to his platoon, especially when they were pinned down at a tactical disadvantage. Without a word, Soko would pass the commanding officer his firearm and take off into the thick vegetation with nothing but a tonto blade in his palm. When he returned, he would exchange his rifle with the scalps of the enemy, a custom no man challenged. Evidence of this past was stamped on his chest over his heart. A black handprint was tattooed there in the Comanche tradition, a symbol that a warrior had triumphed in hand to hand combat. Those finger tips peeked above the collar of the cheap A-shirt he wore now, almost touching the folds of his weathered neck.

Only his hair had yet to age, a fact he wore proudly like a regal crown. It hung straight and black from his skull like a shiny and luxurious mane. When the strain in his broken limbs become too great, he would bellow and shake, whipping this great tassel to and fro.

When the war ended, Soko returned to his reservation in Oklahoma where he dug a pit in his true nation's ground and burned his uniforms including his dress blues with the chest laden with the cheap medals which melted so easily. He thought he destroyed it all, but found something still remained within him. In an attempt to scorch his insides of the indestructible, he took to roasting his belly with firewater. After a twenty year stupor, he had nearly succeeded in the cremation of his being when a missionary's small boy triumphed where his father had failed. Soko nodded in that boy's direction now, and Byron smiled back.

He stoically and expertly sized up the match between Mackey and Chris in one quick glance. "Good, Chris. Now, pull his left arm toward the mat."

Chris obeyed and Mackey grunted in pain an

instant before tapping the mat. Chris released him to do a victory dance around the mat.

"You just got schooled by a seventh grader who eats pop tarts and fruit rollups for breakfast," Archie taunted.

Soko corrected, "It is not about size or strength. It is about technique. Jiu Jitsu was created so little Jap women could defend themselves from rape against big samurai."

"You hear that, Mack? You're never getting laid in Japan," Archie added, settling on the mat next to Mackey.

Soko continued, "The same applies to stand up. The fighter with the better technique can defeat the stronger man. This is what I want to go over today."

Mackey elbowed Archie. "Better pay attention, Little-Big Man."

Soko tossed Chris a pair of white boxing gloves

emblazoned with an American flag logo. Mackey moved to help Chris lace them up, but then paused. "Where did you get these gloves, Soko? They say made in Pakistan!"

Archie grabbed the other glove and examined it. "Yeah, he's right. All this time we've been punching each other in the face with these and they're probably filled with anthrax."

Recognizing the jovial mood of his fighters, Soko put them back on task. "Forget the gloves. Let's talk about Dirty Boxing. It is like wrestling, only standing up. Muhammad Ali did this often."

"You talking low blows and rabbit punches?" Mackey asked.

"No, that's street fighting stuff. This is a way of boxing that gives you control over your opponent. It is only dirty because it is sneaky...if you do it right."

Mackey, usually interested in indirect methods, was skeptical. "No offense, Soko, but it sounds like a waste of time."

"I already went over it with Chris. You have fifty pounds on him. Let's say you go a round with him and see what happens."

Mackey addressed Chris and he pulled on some gloves. "Okay, but I don't want your mom bitching at me if I knock you out, young Grasshopper."

As Chris and Mackey began to spar, Mackey had the immediate advantage. He smirked with over confidence, feeling he was getting the better of both Soko and Chris the same bout. Archie was more interested in studying Chris, and he could discern something like distraction on the boy's face…no, not distraction, but focus as he recalled what Soko had taught him. Then, swiftly and suddenly, Chris had Mackey against the wall, slipping in close range jabs and stiff uppercuts. Mackey tried to pivot out of the way which opened him up to a straight cross from Chris. He fell to a knee and raised his other arm in surrender.

Archie clapped his hands. "What happened, Mackey? That's twice today the kid got you!"

Mackey tried to stand up, but thought better of it and crawled off the mat. "I take back what I said, Soko. It's good. Try it out, Arch," he said pulling his gloves off and tossing them to Archie.

Archie ruffled Chris's hair. "Okay, Chris. Give me what you got. I know you took it easy on Mackey on account of his being delicate, but you don't have to hold back with me."

Archie did well against Chris initially, almost without effort until he caught a quick hook to the head. The blow was not especially hard, and for a moment Archie actually smiled, rubbing his temple with a glove. "Damn, you got me, kid..."

Then he grabbed his skull with both gloves as he stumbled back a few paces before sprawling out on the mat, unconscious.

As Soko and Byron leaned over him, trying to wake him, his own fall caused the dog tags to swing from the cross. They read:

JEANNOPOULOS

ACHILLES J.

U.S. ARMY

A-POSITVE

GREEK ORTHODOX

CHAPTER EIGHT

Byron nervously chewed the upper part of his full Manchu as he fervently read the Bible, moving his lips to the words as he hunched in an uncomfortable chair. He could have quoted nearly every line of the holy book, but he was reading it now as a form of prayer.

For him, the world existed in two halves: the physical and the spiritual. Every so often, a being was born who could conceptualize the physical world in their mind, divining the theories of gravity, particles and light. Few could match their intelligence enough to understand these geniuses, let alone disprove their hypotheses. Most didn't even try, but accepted these superior intellects and trusted themselves to these insights with an assured faith. Most of humanity knew how to board a plane, but not many could explain even half the principals involved with mechanized flight. They had faith in a science that surpassed their own comprehension. There was another kind of genius which fell to earth with similar frequency. Spiritual geniuses who saw the spiritual world in a way that was beyond the ability of all others. Their followers had to also rely on a vision that surpassed their own. Jesus could have been such a man, and like Socrates or Galileo, he was persecuted for having an acumen beyond others.

So absorbed was Byron in the text of his spiritual guru, he didn't notice had Archie woken in the hospital bed next to him. He groggily took in his surroundings, becoming quietly aggravated to find himself hospitalized. He hated hospitals. His medical record would be pulled and he would become a ghost, haunted and transparent. The practitioners could see his prior service and he would be asked questions. Do you have trouble sleeping? Feelings of depression? How often do you drink? And he would lie, not for the sake of deceit, but because lectures were not a cure for what he had seen and done.

When at last his aching eyes fell upon his exhausted bedside friend, his heart lifted. He muttered, "I hope this isn't Heaven."

Bryon slapped the Bible shut. "Welcome back, brother."

"Man, the hospital! Are you trying to get me sick?"

"There he is. You've been out for a while. All day, Arch."

"Really? Well…fuckin' dirty boxing, huh?"

"Yeah, dirty boxing. Chris feels horrible about it."

"Nah, that's stupid. This stuff happens. You tell him that?"

"I did, I did. But I think he'll like it a lot better when it's coming from you. Scared us, man. I mean, when you didn't come to after a minute or two… That's weird. You should have come back."

"Yeah, guess so," Archie said as he peered under his blanket. "You know, it doesn't matter how many times I wake up in a strange bed without my underwear, I'm always surprised."

"All right, brother. I'll go see if I can find your clothes," Bryon said, relieved to be laughing instead of worrying as he rose from his chair. As he exited the room a bald doctor in a white coat entered and took his seat.

"Mr. Jeannopoulous...am I saying that right?"

"Eh, close enough, Doc. Nobody gets it right."

"Well, what I have to tell you is not the easiest thing to hear. I'm just going to be very direct. For six hours we were unable to wake you…this is significant. Anything over six hours is generally considered a state of coma."

"Shit. The kid's first knockout and he hits me

into a coma."

"Albeit it a short one, but a coma nonetheless. This prompted me to order an MRI to further examine your condition, you understand?"

"So far, so good."

"I believe the blow to the head you sustained during training upset a medulloblastoma that has formed in your skull…well, on your brain to be precise. This caused you to have a seizure, followed by the loss of consciousness."

Archie naturally tried to place the word in Greek… medulloblastomas? He had heard blastomas, his mother used that word before, but where? Ah, yes, in the garden. She was talking about the sprouted tomatoes which were growing fast, burgeoning…As Archie did his linguistic recall, Dr. Cavanaugh stood in silence, scrutinizing the sluggish response as a possible indicator of mental enfeeblement. Finally, Archie asked, "A medulloblastoma? I speak a little Greek, but not that much."

"Oh, I'm not very good at switching from doctor talk to patient talk, Mr. Jeannopoulos, and I apologize," Dr. Cavanaugh said, feeling ashamed at his habit of treating patients like subjects of study rather than fellow human beings, a practice manifested from a decade of medical school. He continued, "Basically, it is located on the cerebellum of your brain. It's a kind of tumor."

PARIS

"A tumor?"Archie inquired, squirming in the bed as though to face the invader before coming to the full realization that the intrusion was within.

"Yeah... I mean, yes, it's brain cancer, I'm afraid. To be honest, it's clear from the MRI results alone, but even still, I took a sample of your cerebrospinal fluid and…I'm sorry."

Cancer? Archie bit his lip to fight back the urge

to use wild profanity. He felt like someone who had taken their car in for an oil change only to have the mechanic tell them now they needed a whole new engine. He had always feared even mild ailments because for him it was the true unknown. He had never been ill, not even with chickenpox, a fact his mother credited to an early diet of breast milk instead of formula. The sickest he had ever been was from a hangover following a New Year's Eve party that lasted until the third of January, but that had been self-induced and worth it. A lifetime of being impervious to illness only to be so mortally inflicted was a terrible irony to reconcile.

Coming to terms with the problem, Archie was already trying to solve it. "So what happens now? I guess we have to remove it?"

"I'm afraid that's not a viable option. We can't remove it, without removing vital parts of your brain, and even then, some of it would still be there and continue to grow."

"So what? I mean, how long do I have? What am I supposed to do here?"

"The truth is, anything I say is just my best guess. You need to know that this is a very aggressive, mean cancer. I think, the best course of action is to begin chemotherapy right way. I mean, tonight. I really do believe if we begin to treat this now, we can significantly slow down the growth and extend your life expectancy exponentially."

Extend his life? The very thought forbade the imminence of his fate, the inevitable end to his mortality gaining an encroaching, definitive date. Archie had always had a feeling of impending doom, a consciousness of his mortality that went beyond the human condition. He didn't dwell on it, yet it reflected in his lack of investments. He never really believed he would never live to see the recompense of a 401k or feel arthritis in well used bones. Yet, he would have thought this destiny of a youthful death to be fulfilled on a foreign battlefield, not in a hospital bed wearing a dress.

"I've been getting headaches...just thought it was from fighting. What is it going to be like? I mean, what is it going to do to me? What can I expect?"

"You mean, as the cancer progresses?"

Archie nodded, struggling to understand this new foe. He had embraced the directness of fighting corps a corps, body to body, in the cage. Now he was being attacked as though from a faraway archer, out of range of his ability to grasp and counter, wounded on vital hinge upon which his whole being depended lest it topple to the ground never to rise again.

"As the tumor grows, it will create pressure between your skull and brain. The brain is incredibly complex so it is difficult to know what parts will be affected for sure."

Archie could see the doctor holding back.

"Just...I'm a soldier, okay? A fighter, a tough guy. You can give it to me straight, ok? Please."

"Alright. The headaches will definitely persist. We can give you medicine for that. You will probably experience nausea and imbalance if you haven't already. You may have memory loss, hallucinations, fluctuations in your mood...it's just very difficult to know what will happen for sure."

"Can I go home tonight?"

"You are still a free citizen so you can do what you want. But it would be my strongest recommendation that you stay here until arrangements can be made for a live-in aide. As I said, it is very hard to predict how and when this will affect you. You need rest, and you need to be careful. Even the slightest bump to the head could rupture the tumor. This would be deadly. You understand?"

Archie nodded and a moment of silence passed, the Doctor standing mute by his bedside the same way he would next to his bunk in bootcamp when Taps played, acknowledging death.

"Oh, one more thing. You really shouldn't drive anymore. It just wouldn't be worth the risk."

Byron entered the room carrying Archie's clothes in a bag as Dr. Cavanaugh left.

"The nurses were fighting over your boxers, stud. Was that the doctor? What'd he say?"

"Eh, he said it was just a fluke. Freak accident. Nothing to worry about, man. Now let's get out of here. I bet they charge a hundred bucks a minute to rent the bed."

CHAPTER NINE

The day had cooled into a damp evening by the time Bryon pulled the car up to the church. Archie was sullen in the passenger seat, lost in thought and made no move when Byron put the car in park.

"You feeling all right, brother?"

"I'm just tired, Byron."

"You slept all day!"

"Not that kind of tired."

"What kind of tired then?"

"Not the kind that sleep can mend," Archie said with a grave weariness in his dejected voice. He was being hit with a weighty exhaustion which was aging him years by the moment. His gaze avoided the passenger side mirror, for he felt sure he would see his skin weather and his hair thin before his eyes.

Byron observed him and recognized a familiar disposition. Even the best fighters needed the minute between rounds to catch their breath, but often the stresses of life gave no such reprieve. "Ah, I see...well, I've got to be honest with you, I don't know any fighters that had an easy life. Any one that was ever any good came from a hard place. You're a real fighter, Archie."

Archie thought to tell him about the cancer, to throw the same curveball into Byron's pep talk that he himself had been pitched. He thought better of it. His own thinking was clouded and he needed his friend's acuity unfettered. He sighed. "I was thinking about what Bob said in his sermon. About life and God given purpose. If we each have a purpose, why doesn't God just tell us exactly what it is? See, God probably is a woman. Expects us all to be mind readers."

"What do you call the whole Jesus coming to earth thing? God has told us what to do."

"Nah, that's too general. I'm talking about *my* purpose and *your* purpose. The reason that each of us is even here."

Bryon pat Archie on the leg and cocked his head in a, "let's go" motion as he exited the vehicle. He stood against the car and lit a cigarette while Archie sat on the church steps.

"I've been in the fight business a long time, Archie. When I was a fighter, it was never about the fight, or the other guy. I wasn't trying to prove anything to the crowd or even God. It was about me. Looking for something, trying to prove something to myself. Now that I'm a manager I see the same thing in all my fighters. This searching within. And it's given me my own theory about God and purpose."

"Share your wisdom. Maybe you can save me a few black eyes."

"I think we were once all souls in Heaven, before we came here, to this life. And we came here not because God forced us, but because we asked Him to send us here."

"Why would anyone want to leave Heaven? I thought that's what we're supposed to be working towards in the first place."

"You ever notice how miserable retired people are? They worked hard their whole lives for the golden years just to wish they were back doing whatever it is they were doing before. You see, they miss having purpose, they miss being challenged and proving themselves. You get it? I think we begged God to send us here because we wanted - no, needed to prove something, not to Him, but to ourselves.

"Prove what though?"

"Everyone wants different things. Some people may want to prove that they are compassionate or brave or generous, so they asked God to design a life that would test them for those things."

"Ask and you shall receive, huh?"

"Exactly, brother. But the kicker is, for any of that to work, God had to take our knowledge of Him away. Otherwise, nothing we did would be a challenge, nothing would require faith. It would be like playing poker and knowing all the cards."

"Well, I'm a fool now and I must have been a fool then, because whatever I asked God for has been a real kick in the ass."

"You know what I've always loved about you?"

"I don't know. Probably my great hair."

"When you say, "eh." It's like a life philosophy with you. Something bad happens, and I always hear you say, "eh" and you don't let it stick to you. You don't let it tarnish you. You just go on trying to do the right thing anyways. If I had my guess, I'd say you asked God to make you an honorable man, because that's way I see you."

"Whatever this life is about, I'm glad we met,

brother. I don't like many people." Archie said this regretfully, for too often he had witnessed human beings offend the very title. They behaved more like bald monkeys, deliberately dumb to the world to remain spiritually blind, intellectually deaf and morally mute. It took two hands to tear the world apart. One hand rejecting every truth while the other embraced every lie. His greatest hope was that in another millennia or so, an emerged mankind would look back at his day and call it a second Dark Age. Before Byron could persuade him towards broader compassion, he was halted by Archie's phone chiming repeatedly from inside the car where it had been charging. Bryon reached in through the open window and tossed it to Archie.

"Man, Meaghan was blowing up my phone while I was out."

"Oh yeah, she called me while you were out processing. She was worried about you. Not a bad girl to have in your corner, Arch."

"I'm starting to see that. I gotta bounce man, but thanks for taking care of me today. Tell Chris I'm going to kick his ass."

Archie pulled his leather jacket from Byron's car and used it to wipe the dew off his motorcycle seat before hopping on.

"All right man, just remember, tomorrow is a new day."

Archie stood in his seat to give Bryon a hug.

Under his breath as he started the motorcycle he whispered, "That's what I'm afraid of.

CHAPTER TEN

Archie leaned against the side of the brick building of the motorcycle dealership, gazing at his metal steed through dark aviators. It was a cloudy day, but he wore the glasses to hide his eyes which felt wet, each covered in a solitary tear which refused to break and coated the surface of his pupils as a thick lens. Those two wheels had given him the speed he needed to flee from the beautiful and tormenting ghosts that pursued him elsewhere, as though they couldn't keep up with the wind in his hair.

The bells on the glass door next to him jingled as the salesman stepped out and passed him a check, saying, "How's that look?"

Archie didn't bother to look before stuffing it into his back pocket. There was no amount of zeros that would dull the pain of this departure. He started to reply, but his throat felt tight, so he just nodded instead. He had known there would come a day he couldn't ride anymore, but he hadn't expected it so soon. To lose consciousness or equilibrium on the motorcycle would be to splatter the tumor inside his skull across the asphalt. He took one last look at his beloved bike as a mechanic wheeled it away.

***

The rusty shocks of the old mustang squeaked as Archie drove it across the potholes of the uneven marina parking lot. It had cost him the price of his motorcycle and still needed work, but he knew this was his last chance to make good on his desires towards this car. Yet, even as he closed the door the gratification of the purchase still hadn't settled in. The line between wanting to do a thing and having to do it had been crossed.

As he walked toward the boathouse, the purples and yellows of a flower bed caught his eye. He knelt in front of the assembly of flora, taken aback by their symmetrical beauty, more over astonished that he went past every day without ever noticing. Caressing a yellow one, he plucked it for a closer look and immediately regretted it. Why had he done that, killed it just for being beautiful?

He continued his walk, under the boathouse and onto the worn wood of the dock, feeling remorse for the slain foliage in his hand. As he neared the water, the pink and red of the sunset tinted all. This was not a piece of nature he had overlooked. In fact, he made a point to leave indoors during this time every day. The thought struck him now that he had a finite number of opportunities left to admire such a view. The moon was already hanging in the sky, sharing canvas with the falling sun while the few remaining rose colored clouds crossed almost imperceptibly slow, yet carried enough momentum to budge his heavy heart inside his chest. Since his diagnosis the day before, he had thought of nothing but his own demise, but those thoughts of death had given birth to an awareness of fleeting life. Everything seemed to be alive around him, the flowers, the water and the sky…but soon he would no longer be a part of that circle of life. Any day now, he would be plucked from it like the flower in his hand. Archie felt the thick cataract of a tear that he had carried as an ocular weight throughout the day finally break, falling from the steep surface of his eyes and cascading down the curves of his cheeks as he bereaved himself.

CHAPTER ELEVEN

He woke the next day much later than usual. Sleeping past nine on a boat was usually made difficult as the rising sun cooked the fiberglass hull, but today it was Olive's purposeful whining that stirred him from his slumber. He didn't really want to wake up, to face the day as a new version of himself which was terminally ill.

Normally, he would train his body for the cage, but that seemed like a moot point now. As a self-disciplined, militant man, he was suddenly lost without his daily routine. His responsibilities had shifted with the diagnosis and arrangements had to be made for treatment. Worse than that, he had to tell people. The burden was so great it was easier to drop the load altogether, to forgo the task and reclaim some control over the situation by refusing to participate in the unwelcome drama.

In an attempt to use his physicality for a

constructive purpose and distract his mind, he took to working on the mustang. Archie mused that in its decrepit state, the car was not just old, but in fact elderly, for while the classic interior was refined, it was the exterior which was so terribly worn.

He spent the day banging dents out of the body and repairing corroded patches of rust. Now he was sanding the surface smooth, preparing for paint. He was in a decent mood, a combination of the music coming from the cab, the beer on ice in the trunk and the masculine satisfaction of mastering the physical world around him, even just in this automotive project.

He wore a torn olive drab, ball cap which was embroidered with, "IRAQ-AFGHANISTAN VETERAN" which he doffed to wipe the sweat from his brow. The heat of the midday sun had passed, but the work perspired him. Thirsty, he pulled another beer from the trunk, aware that he was rather drunk and intending to get drunker still.

Ears perking at the snap and hiss of another beer opening, Olive glanced expectantly at him with begging eyes. Archie shook his head mid sip, but then relented, kneeling down to caress the loyal companion and pour a portion of the brew into her bowl. "Okay, doe eyes, you've talked me into it."

As Olive lapped up the beer, it was Archie who heard the familiar rumbling of an approaching car in dire need of a new exhaust system. Meaghan was talking before she was even all the way out of the tired automobile. "Hey, Soldier, how are you holding up?"

"I'm using my dick like a tripod."

"Guess I walked right into that one."

Archie staggered drunkenly and threw his arms open. "Walk right into this."

Meaghan embraced him and his scent of beer and sweat. She rubbed her cheek on the soft fabric hugging his chest, relishing how deliciously soft all of his clothes were from overuse and exposure to the sea. He felt like the well-worn rope which secured the Argo to the dock, worn down by the elements but proven strong daily. Then she peered curiously over his shoulder. "So...this is the car?"

"Yeah, what do you think? I mean, she'll look better with some new paint."

Meaghan smiled at Archie's tendency to personify his vehicles, the more high maintenance ones usually as women. It wasn't misogynistic, quite the contrary, he couldn't help saving what he saw as distressed maidens.

"Nah, I know. I like it, so long as you'll still take me out on the motorcycle now and again."

"I'm not made of money, woman! I had to sell the bike to get this."

"Wow. That's...really hard to believe. You loved

that bike, said you'd never give it up. You bought it with the last of your deployment money."

"It's not a big deal, Meg." Archie shrugged but avoided Meaghan's gaze, a move she knew signified he was feeling contrary to his words.

"I guess. It's out of character though," she said, digging. She was bewildered by his sudden apathy towards his most prized of possession. Meaghan was pondering the psychological implications of Archie's abrupt defiance of his own personality while he leaned in through the mustang window to retrieve the cigarette lighter which popped in the ashtray. Her face fell as he pulled a cigarette from behind his ear and pressed the burning coil to the tobacco, inhaling sensuously.

"You're smoking?"

"Right back at you, Babe."

"Not cool, Archie. You know that causes cancer, right?"

"You don't say?"

Archie chuckled, amused by the joke only he was privy to, which only peeved Meaghan more than the noxious fumes.

"Yeah, it's horrible. You're a fighter, what are you even thinking?"

"Nope, not anymore. I'm done with fighting."

"And with thinking, apparently. You're just drunk."

"Who are you, the drunk police?"

"That's the normal police...You're really done with fighting? What did Byron say about that?"

Archie popped open another beer, clumsily spilling another portion into Olive's dog dish.

"Haven't told him yet. Doesn't matter. I want to enjoy what life I have left."

"Huh. So smoking and getting drunk with your dog at three p.m. is you enjoying life?"

"Hey, take it easy! She's twenty-one in dog years. And what if it is, Meaghan?"

"Then that's pretty sad. That's not the Archie I know, and I've got to think there is something else happening here." Meaghan knew there was always a reason behind unusual behavior, and it seemed to her Archie was avoiding a difficult situation.

He recognized her attempt to analyze him and rolled his eyes condescendingly. "Hey Princess, do me a solid and maybe finish the psychology degree before you start applying it."

"It's called an education. Maybe you should get one before you belittle mine."

"Please, little girl. I can treat a tension pneumothorax while calling for a medevac and returning fire. I'm plenty educated."

"Maybe you need to go somewhere where no one is trying to kill you. Study abroad."

"I study broads all the time."

"You know, whatever. I don't know why you're suddenly giving up your health, your bike, or fighting. All the things you love it seems. I just hope you don't give up on everything you care about so easily."

Archie began to sand the car again to show he was disinterested even though she was right. Those were the things he loved and his heart was breaking to give them up. What else could there possibly be that he had left to give up now? So he asked, without really wanting to know, "Like what?"

"You know what."

Oh, that. Romance. The beer and the subject made him belligerent. He was facing death and was still expected to deal with her emotional wants. He had given her as much of him as was available, and still she was feeling rebuffed.

"Christ, Meg, I literally don't have the time left

in this world to molly coddle your vast array of feelings."

"Fuck you, you, you-fucker," Meaghan stormed back towards her car. How could he throw that in her face? Had he no idea how much she was holding back?

Archie watched her go, torn between going after her and grabbing another beer. He crouched down and stoked Olive's fur, whispering in her ear, "I swear, you're the only girl that gets me."

Yet, even as he said it, he knew it wasn't true but he wasn't ready to tell Meaghan that. It was easier to taunt her than admit that now.

"Oh, look who's giving up now! Yep, run away, Sweetheart!"

Meaghan did an about face and marched back towards Archie, furious to see his cocky smirk and determined to remove it. She slapped him full across the face feeling the satisfying sting on her own palm and hearing the sharp clap. Archie, who was punched in the face on a daily basis, was amused rather than assaulted, yet would not be handled so roughly without responding in kind. He smacked her back, not hard, almost playfully but Meaghan recoiled dramatically from the strike, struck worse by the shock of it.

"You hit me! I'm a woman!"

"I don't discriminate, you sexist pig."

"You're incredible!"

"Finally, something we agree on."

At a loss for words, she cuffed him again, turning for her car immediately after to avoid a repeat reprisal. Before she was too far away, Archie slapped her back, this time on her ass.

Grinning, he called after her, "What is your problem?"

She whirled around and took a few quick paces back towards Archie, who mockingly bobbed and weaved as though getting ready to spar.

"You! You're my problem! We've been doing, whatever this is for a while now, and I've been great to you. I know you've got your issues. And that's fine. Hey, no pressure. I don't have to be your everything yet, but I can't be nothing to you anymore because you're something to me, Archie!"

Archie's face fell, recognizing the sincerity in her voice and regretting his taunts. She had been good to him. She deserved to know the truth about the cancer, or at least that he was not apathetic to her. He took a step towards her, reaching a hand for hers but she batted it away.

"Meaghan, look..."

"I'm in love with an asshole! That's my problem!"

"Listen, I can't..."

"That about sum it up, Champ?"

She gave him no chance for reply before stomping off to her car. Archie turned away, picked up a beer can and finding it empty, flung the empty tin vessel, thoroughly pissed off. He picked up the sanding block and took his frustration out on the car.

He wasn't expecting to see Meaghan's car still there when he looked up. He rose, seeing now the reason for her delay in going. She was crying and so upset she was fumbling to get the key in the ignition. He softened to see her distraught beyond such routine coordination, recalling the night he stumbled drunk through a field. It was dark so that he did not notice the small Bluejay laid in the grass until his heavy foot found it. It let out a terrified chirp before his weight crushed it's small bones. It was still alive, so he moved quickly, using the whisky bottle in his hand to end the pain he had caused. The remorse he felt was doubled the next day, when rediscovering the carcass, another Bluejay dive bombed him, coming half an inch from his head as it bravely defended what was left of its mate. To have crushed something so lovely, slight and innocent was not a blunder he wished to repeat.

He neared the car and as he reached to open the door, she pushed in the door stem lock. Archie only sighed and reached in through the open window to pull the lock up. He opened the door, and taking her by the shoulders with carefully applied force, he stood her up against the car. Leaning in close, he said, "I happen to have a similar problem with this beautiful pain in the ass I know."

By her expression alone, Archie knew she was going to tell him some version of, "screw you," so he stifled her mouth with his own before she could utter it. She only relented mid-kiss.

Then Archie pulled away with a puzzled expression an instant before his knee's buckled and he fell to the ground, sliding along Meaghan's car to break his fall. He had felt the icy numbness rise from his heel, up his calves to his thighs…and then he felt nothing below the waist. Now, slumped against the car, he realized he was paralyzed below the waist, yet the tingling in his toes assured him it was just a momentary collapse.

"Archie? Are you okay? What's wrong?" Meaghan said, crouching beside him in alarm.

"You're a terrible kisser," Archie groaned.

"I'll have you know that opinion differs from the general consensus. Stop being an ass. What's going on with you?"

Archie tested out his legs, finding them improved yet still failing, resulting in a second collapse which prompted Olive to rush to his side, licking his face in concern.

Meaghan pulled her phone from her pocket. "I'm

calling someone."

"No, just...look, Meaghan. I'm Greek. I do three things well. I fight, I cook and make love. Now that I'm done fighting with you tonight, let's get dinner the hell out of the way."

CHAPTER TWELVE

Meaghan studied Archie as he cooked, humming along to Greek bouzouki music as though he hadn't been a helpless heap only moments before.

"I want to know, Archie. You're not going to wine and dine me out of this one."

"Ah, that's right, the wine," he said, seizing a bottle and holding a glass to Meaghan as he pulled the cork with his teeth. She stubbornly crossed her arms, refusing to take the proffered cup. Archie continued to press her, by waving the glass under her nose as he poured. She snatched it from his hand, but didn't drink. Archie gestured emphatically for her to partake. She finally took an appeasing sip before pressing the glass back into Archie's hand. "Yep, I still want to know."

"You're really going to bust my balls on this?"

"You better believe it."

Archie returned his attention towards the

cooking pot, the contents of which were bubbling over the sides and hissing in instant evaporation on the hot burner. He placated the boiling liquid by stirring it with a wooden spoon and sighed realizing Meaghan had been so agitated, and unfortunately he would have to stir her now to keep her from bubbling over.

"Alright, cancer. I have cancer, Meaghan." The words rang in his own ears like an off note.

"That's not funny, Archie."

"Yeah, my delivery was all wrong."

"I'm serious."

"So am I."

Meaghan desperately searched his face for a sign a gest, hoping that if she looked at him long enough the answer would change like a vagrant who has just spent their last dollar on a losing scratch off.

"Oh my God. You are! What kind of cancer is it?"

Archie raised his eyebrows and tapped his head. For a moment, Meaghan was puzzled, but her academic brain made the quick connection. The mind and its organ would soon become her professional bailiwick and while she was not an oncologist, she had studied the cognitive effects associated with brain tumors in preparation for making early diagnoses. She felt immediate guilt and failure at not having done so here. "This is terrible!" she cried.

"I know. It would have at least been nice if it were testicular. Would've explained that situation."

"How can you be so nonchalant about this?"

Archie only shrugged his shoulders. "Eh."

"What are the doctors saying?"

"You know...there was actually some pretty bad news, Meg."

At Archie's somber response, Meaghan threw her arms around him. He grabbed her sweet smelling hair, inhaling it. The human contact felt good and for a moment he rejoiced at finally sharing the grave news with another. He began to choke up, but then feeling selfish for the indulgence, swallowed the rock in his throat and clenched his jaw to steel himself. Meaghan trembled in his arms, terrified for him. He couldn't bear to impart the finality of his infliction to her, to wound her farther. As he composed himself, a wry smile began to form.

"Well, apparently, I'm too old to be an eligible candidate for the Make-a-Wish Foundation."

Meaghan pulled away, confused as she wiped a tear from her eye. "Huh?

Archie's grin served as the punchline to the joke.

"Oh, you son of..." She playfully hit him even as she released a laugh of relief.

"Could you imagine, Make-a-Wish at the Playboy Mansion?"

"Seriously Arch, what happens next?"

"I don't know, I've never had cancer before. I guess they want me to start a combination of chemo and radiotherapy soon."

"Okay, okay. Well, when are you going in for that? I want to take you."

Archie turned the burner off slowly, mesmerized by the flames licking the hot spokes as they retreated through the grate's middle. "I don't think I'm going in for that, Meaghan." He understood that the cancer was a many headed hydra and to lop off one head would only spawn two in its place. Each had to be severed and the oozing neck quickly cauterized by a burning torch…but if this method slayed such an indomitable monster, how could he survive it?

"I just don't see how radiation cures cancer. If that works, why don't they just give people radioactive vitamins every day to stop it in the first place?"

"No, Archie, no, you have to go. Don't even say that you won't. Please? You have to fight this." Her pleading was another reason Archie did not want to share his dismal prognosis. He wasn't so attached to life that he was willing to wither away in a hospital bed, clutching desperately to it. He knew few in the Western world would understand that and didn't want to be pressured into enduring such a protracted demise. His life was a series of crude struggles and the novelty of short lived triumphs had worn off some time ago.

"I'm tired of fighting, Meg. I've fought in two wars for countries that weren't even mine, and once a week I'm locked in a steel cage with some animal that wants to tear me apart for sport. And that I do for God. My profession in life has been war!"

"You are choosing her over me."

"What are talking about?"

"Diane. You don't care about dying because you

miss her and you think you'll see her."

Archie felt the skin of his face tighten as his ears fell back like a lion whose territory had been encroached. "Watch it. God, I shouldn't have told you anything."

"It's the truth. You'd rather die for her than live for me."

"Bravo, Meaghan, you've made this about you. Freakin' egomaniac."

"Spare me, that's the pot calling the kettle black."

"Wait, why am I the pot in that scenario? I mean, I'm the one that goes around like this..." Archie flexed his bicep, knuckles pointing away from him in a classic body building pose. With his other arm on his hip, he tilted like a teapot with a self-amused smile on his face.

"THAT is exactly what I mean! You're so full of

yourself!"

"Hey, if you were full of me, you'd be smiling too," Archie quipped, not offended for he knew it was true…at least from the outside looking in. Sure, he was an egoist but he was also a cynic, believing all were essentially in the pursuit of their own selves, not just him. This was an essential fact of his existence, for before he could know the world, he had to first know himself. He recognized he was the center of his universe, for to assume anything more was to pretend to be God, omnipotent and all seeing, more capable of affecting change in the world around him than he actually was…an egoist out of proportion with reality: a true egomaniac. His mere mortal vision extended from himself to a limited range. Yet he was King of his life, interchangeably benevolent or tyrannical as it suited him, his actions requiring no justification to another. The history of others was of less real relevance to him than his own, which was *his story*. The irony was that this fundamental insight to his own nature inspired him to counter the human drive towards self-perpetuation by acknowledging it in his mind rather than exercising it in it his actions. It was those who presumed to be altruistic and kind that usually made no efforts towards the actual practice, for it was those who were not self-aware who were truly self-possessed.

"Archie!" Meaghan snapped him out of his brevity of self-reflection. "You're going to die if you don't do anything, you realize that?"

"I'll meet my fate when God delivers it."

"That's selfish. What about those of us who love you, Arch? We have to keep on living after you go, and with holes in our hearts. I know you miss, Diane. I don't take it personally, she was first. But you know what that kind of loss feels like. Don't do it to us. If there's a chance you can beat this, any chance, even a God damn miracle of a chance, you owe it to us, to take it. If you love me, if you love any of us…you will."

"It's not enough. I've fought for God and country, now you want me to fight for love?"

"I would love you in any country, under any God. Do this for me, Archie. Please."

Archie made a move towards the hatchway to leave, but dropped himself on the gangway steps instead, his head in his hands. God and country. The former demanded he battle his soul against his flesh, while the latter had tasked him to risk both in war. Wars were fought by armies belonging to countries run by governments. Therefore, there could be no war without a nation. Only the strictest atheism and anarchy could spare him the burden of morality and the duty to sanctioned violence. Yet, he could not renounce his citizenship any more than he could his soul.

He was not as unfettered as he liked to believe,

nor could he deny that Meaghan had a point. There were people who cared about him, who deserved better. He yearned for his boyhood days, when right and wrong appeared to him as black and white. The first time he had felt so morally divided was on his first tour in Iraq when a detainee in a yellow jumpsuit curled at his feet on the floor of a cell coated with the grey, left over paint from a Navy ship. Archie was still just a kid, yet this bearded man was crying real tears of agony, begging Archie to allow him to defecate. The rules of that cell block were purposely strict, not unlike Archie's boot camp training, and the detainees were allowed only one visit to the latrine a day. Archie followed his orders, denying the detainee by cruelly screaming at him without outward pity as he had been instructed. Yet as his own eyes obscured with tears, the yellow detainee disappeared and all Archie saw was the grey paint of the cell. Ever since, the world no longer appeared black and white and his soul felt compromised and morality hazy. As he looked up at Meaghan, the concern in her eyes allowed the uncomfortable truth to saturate him. He knew there was no way he could proceed without medical care and not feel guilty.

"I don't want to die like this, Meg. Always thought I'd die fighting. A warrior's death. Not this."

Meaghan was taken aback by the uncharacteristic dejection in Archie's form and voice. She had felt sure he had such moments, but had always taken pains to hide such sorrows from others behind a smart remark and easy smile. She dropped to her knees in front of him, placing her hands on his shoulders, unsure what she was going to say. Her studies recommended advising distressed patients by putting their problems into a perspective they could understand.

"This is a fight, Arch. The fight of your very life. You made it through two wars and God knows how many cage fights and you can make it through this. Maybe others can't, but you can."

Meaghan felt the conviction which grew in her words as she spoke accompanied by a measure of relief as Archie nodded his assent. "Okay. I'll go, but just the chemo...I'm already radiant."

"I can take you tomorrow. In the morning?"

"No, there's somethings I need to do first. Give me a day, then I'll go."

CHAPTER THIRTEEN

Archie signed the receipt and picked up the paper bag off the drug store counter, which rattled like a maraca with the various bottles of pills his doctor had prescribed. Passing a garbage can, he paused, fished the half empty bottle of aspirin from his black denim jacket and tossed it in the trash.

"Hope you're not getting sick, slick," Joe said, announcing his presence from his seat at the automatic blood pressure machine. "Fighting is only fun if you're strong."

Archie pointed to the mechanically constricting band on Joe's arm. "Huh, go figure, you've got a heart."

Joe snickered, "Yeah, heard you got one too and it's all sweet on the pole worker gal…Meaghan, right?"

"You trying to know my business, Joe? You got a fuckin' crush on me or something?"

"Thing is, I've lost my best girl. Got herself

knocked up by some deadbeat like you. I gotta keep some nice ass in the VIP, special customers, you know? Anyways, hope you don't mind her working for me. Hell, I'll have her give you a lap dance on the house even."

"Like hell, you guinea prick."

Joe's blood boiled at the slight, causing the machine to beep rapidly at the sudden vascular escalation. It wasn't the verbiage Archie used. Joe was old enough to let such insults roll off of him like water on a goose's back. It was that someone half his years had the nerve to talk down to him, to assume a position to defy him. His age was an accumulation of time which Joe had endured to acquire a level of power in the small town, and Archie ought to respect that. "Hey, who the fuck are you to talk to me like that? Huh? Cocky punk. People may like to see you fight, but they come to *my* club to pay *me* for the privilege. I'm king around here, not you."

"King of a bunch of bloody thirsty drunks and club skanks. Besides, I'm done fighting at your two bit dive all together."

"What?" Joe impulsively tried to rise from the calculating machine, which whirred in protest. "You going to quit fighting over some girl? Don't be ridiculous."

"Good luck finding any quality fighters, Joe. You'll be begging to have me back."

"Doesn't have to be that way. I tell you what, kid, you take Heckman on, and I'll make do without her. How's that sound?"

"See? You've already started."

Joe tugged his arm out of the band and started to follow Archie out, but he was already gone. He looked back at the digital read out on the machine which reset an instant before he could mentally imprint the numbers.

He cursed himself as he sat back in the chair to repeat

the entire process. Under his breath he mumbled, "Of all

the crowd favorites, I hate that son of bitch the most."

CHAPTER FOURTEEN

Archie was about to descend the short flight of stairs to the church basement when he noticed a shoe untied. He crouched before the steps and picked up the two laces, forming the usual loops and then paused, suddenly unsure how to proceed. He stared blankly at his mute hands as a cold sweat tickled his forehead and his heart quickened by the terrifying confrontation of his sudden ineptness…he had forgotten how to tie his shoes. A resentful bitterness quelled his palpitating heart as he recognized with sick irony that the tumor was depriving him of certain memory only after years of him having tried and failed to suppress others.

"Fuck you, shoe," Archie spat as he tied the laces in a square knot, a nautical device used by sailors to hitch two lines.

Byron was stooped over Chris and Mackey, giving them instruction as they grappled. He glanced up and acknowledged Archie with a wink who silently entered the room, folding his arms and leaning against the doorway.

"Nice, now hook his arm with your knee, Chris," Byron advised.

Chris did so, trapping one of Mackey's hands between his bony knees while he pulled the other towards his own shoulder. He was on his back on the mat lying perpendicular to Mackey, like the horizontal beam of a cross. As he plied the hostage's limbs wide apart, his bare stomach provided a sort of pillow for Mackey's head which was turning red as he struggled futilely.

"There it is. The Crucifix," Bryon coached, smiling with pride that his student mastered a new technique. "Look, he can't even tap out," he said pointing to Mackey's hands which flailed uselessly at the wrist. "Ok, well, you can't use a move called the crucifix and have no mercy. Let him up."

Chris released him and rose sheepishly, trying not to show too much pride. He only then noticed Archie propped against the doorway and found he could not meet his eye. Archie strut across the mat towards with pretend aggression in his steps before taking the youth up in a friendly hug.

Archie tousled Chris's shaggy hair. "Don't worry so much, brother. I'm alright! Besides, I should be thanking you. I haven't slept that well in years."

"He's felt like hell about it," Mackey chimed in from his place on the mat.

"I didn't mean to hurt you, you know?"

"Maybe, but fighting is about hurting people and getting hurt. You have to understand that if you're going to last in it. You'll be better for it."

"I mean, it's fighting. I know it hurts people, but I don't know…I didn't like seeing it."

Archie looked to Bryon who was easing into a rusty fold out chair, lighting a cigarette. He gave Archie his nod to proceed with schooling Chris. This acquiescence was his way of acknowledging Byron as the manager, and the nod indicated Byron's approval of Archie's alpha status as the captain of the crew. This subtle ceremony was only necessary because of the close friendship and mutual respect between the two, not in fact, a lack of it.

"In Greek, we have two words for knowledge. One to mean, when you know something because you have been taught, and one for the things you learn from experience. You see Chris, the shift in knowing and realizing happens the moment that knowledge becomes reality. It became real for you the other day. And it was the best training you may ever get." Archie saw this truth in music, particularly the songs he once skipped on the radio which had meant nothing to him long ago, but had developed deep personal meaning from the experiences life had dragged him through.

Chris scratched his head, understanding Archie, but not sure the other understood him. "The thing is, it was extra tough seeing *you* like that. You're the champ, you know?"

Confused, Archie examined the concern on Chris's face. He looked to the others for clarification and a lump rose in his throat when he saw the same thing professed in Byron's slow nod and Mackey's weak smile. They loved him.

With his usual tact in sincere situations, Archie said, "Well, hey, look, get me your mom's phone number and we'll call it square, okay?"

Everyone laughed and the moment was over. Chris wretched, "Fuck, I don't feel bad anymore."

"Yeah, don't feel bad for this guy," Mackey joined in. "Tell him to stuff his Socrates philosophy bull and learn how to fuckin' block."

"Don't listen to him, Chris. The only thing he blocks is his own cock."

"Ok girls, take to the mat. I want to talk to you guys," Bryon ordered.

The three fighters sprawled on the mat as Byron paced a moment before them, stopping to orate. "You know, when I first started training fighters I still did it for free, but I used to have them sign a contract that they'd donate ten percent of their winnings to the church. In this way, I thought I was serving God, but then I realized God doesn't need money! A million dollars doesn't matter anymore to Him than a million cents. It's the giving at all that counts, but by making them sign a contract, I was taking away their chance to give to God of their own volition."

Archie nodded in understanding, though he did not believe that money was the root of all evil, not in and of itself. Rather, it was a want of money which made men commit sin against each other.

For this reason, he did find it therapeutic to give some of his few dollars to a God he knew had no use for it. The act demanded a conversation between his two halves, his spiritual being, who like God, had no use for money, and his human brain that constantly sought the resources of the physical world. The concession of his human being, which dominated reflexively and ruled supreme on a daily basis, empowered his spiritual being to reign from time to time.

Bryon continued, "So now I don't ask you guys to pay anything, but I have to tell you… the church is in trouble."

"What's happening, Byron?" Chris asked.

"You know, we all make mistakes. Bob took a loan out to keep the church going a couple of years ago. A big one. I warned him not to, but he did. Now the bank wants the church or the money back by the end of the week.

"Man, I'm sure Bob meant the best."

"We learn mostly from experience, Chris. You learned that way the other day. Now Bob is learning the same way."

"My Grandfather used to say, a wise man learns from his mistake, but a smart man learns from the mistakes of others."

"Well, the lesson to learn here is, don't take things out on credit. It's evil. It makes you a slave to someone. God said, ask and you shall receive. But he didn't say when, and in today's world we want everything now. We can't wait. When you take things on credit, you are basically saying you don't trust God to give it to you. And then this is the sort of thing that happens."

"Yeah, the American Dream, huh?" Mackey

said sarcastically.

"Now you know why I live on a boat. What do we need to do, Bryon?"

"We need to raise ten grand in five days."

Archie raised his eye brows, surprised by the sum while Chris let out a long whistle.

"Yeah, pretty much."

Mackey scanned the room, puzzled by his companions' dejection. "What's the sweat? We can raise that at the fights. I can take Pat, the Arachnid or whatever he goes by, the chump. That's fifteen hundred right there."

"Still shy eighty-five hundred, Pythagoras."

"And you can fight Heckman for the rest, Archie."

"Get outta here."

"I'm serious. Bryon, you know Joe would pay that much to see it happen. He's busting your hump every week to get these two in the cage."

Byron bit his lip. "I don't like it. We can figure something else out."

"I doubt it. Archie, think about it. The crowd wants you two to duke it out. You two are the titans of that place. And Heckman has gone undefeated for far too long."

"He's undefeated because he outclasses everyone there. He's fighting at a professional level in an amateur club. He'll only take fights he knows he can win because he's a coward."

"If he's a coward, then do it. You don't even need to win the fight, your share of the purse will be enough, with a few side bets."

Archie's blood began to boil at Mackey insistence. Only moments before he had been unable to tie his own shoe. His confidence was rattled and it was difficult enough for a healthy fighter to recall his training when locked in combat. Mackey hadn't seen the same carnage Archie had in war and he lacked the same understanding of just how feeble a construct the human body was, especially in the hands of a steroid fueled sadist. "Mackey, you Irish goon, you fight him! But this ain't a game. This is fighting. Blood and bones, man. There's no way to match him. Besides, I'm done, all right. You may have noticed I didn't dress for training today. I came here to quit."

"Hey, Archie..." Byron began.

"No, I'm serious. I'm done," Archie said, rising from the mat. He had intended to tell them about the cancer, but the look of love and concern on their faces moments before was more than he could face. He was already regretting losing his cool, but the outburst provided the distance he needed to depart without telling the somber truth.

As Archie left the mat, Mackey began to rise to

confront him but Bryon gently pushed him back down with a hand on the shoulder. He motioned for them to stay while he followed Archie out.

***

Archie walked with a purpose towards his usual parking spot only to curse under his breath at his own forgetfulness. He had changed direction and was already near the bus stop on the corner when he heard the familiar footsteps pursuing him.

"I do something wrong, brother?" Byron asked as he came into ear shot.

Archie sighed. He didn't want to have this conversation. "I'm done, Byron. And I'm sorry about the church, I really am. But it's not my fight anymore."

"I hope this isn't about Meaghan. Yeah, Joe told me she'll be shaking it there again."

"It's not that, Bryon."

"Then what? If you're going through something,

you should tell me, because otherwise you're just acting like an asshole."

Archie just shook his head. "I'm sorry I lost it. You tell them that for me. I just can't be a fighter anymore."

"You never were a fighter."

"How can you say that?"

"Because it's true. You're not one of those guys that beats the blood out of someone just for the hell of it. You don't grab the microphone after a fight and pretend that you have emotions about it. Hell, it never even makes a difference to you who you're fighting because you're always fighting the same guy." Byron put a finger to Archie's chest for emphasis. "That's the difference between you and Heckman. His fight is always in the cage. Your fight is always outside the cage...You fight for something more. You have honor, and that makes you a warrior, not a fighter."

He knew Byron intended that as a compliment, and before today, he would have taken it as such. Facing the advance warning of his death had sharpened his perspective on fighting, elucidating the growing notion he had that he was pushing a granite boulder uphill every day, only to have it roll back to the bottom at night, the task never achieved, nothing ever gained.

"There's more to me than that. There are other things I want besides honor. Like peace. That'd be nice. You know, maybe I want to have a child one day too. Yeah, and then I might want to grow old. Fuck, I just want to live, Byron. Can't do that always fighting."

"Look, I never expected you to hang around here forever. I've trained enough fighters to know you've got a bigger battle out there for you, somewhere. But Mackey might be right. We need you, Archie."

Archie felt a tug on his heart to think he was abandoning his friends in a time of distress. Of course, the presence of the cancer made any other choice impossible, and yet that pragmatism took a back seat to Archie's own resolve, which was always total. The city bus squeaked to a stop in front of them, sparing Archie from any further torment. "I'm sorry, brother," he said, disappearing inside the bus.

CHAPTER FIFTEEN

Archie crossed the threshold of the automotive repair shop, a lobby which was an assorted mess of car parts in boxes and racing posters, to ring the bell on the well-worn desk. The place was devoid of life and the usual sounds of mechanics yelling over compressed air wrenches and troubled engines. After a moment, he double checked the hours of operation on the front door and his watch, before ringing the bell once more. He wrapped his knuckles impatiently on the desk, eyes bored into the western style doors which swung into the back room. Finally fed up, he vaulted the desk and pressed the doors apart, scanning the jumbled garage which lay beyond for an employee.

Seeing no one, he scratched his head and turned to leave but then a soft curse brought his attention to the two legs kicking under an old Ford. Coming near, Archie toed one of the oil stained khaki pant legs. There was the sound of a wrench clattering to the cement floor before the mechanic slide from beneath the dilapidated vehicle. Merle, his name printed over his chest, addressed Archie roughly, in the same voice he used to curse at stubborn cars. "You ain't supposed to be back here. It's against policy. You could step on something and hurt yourself."

Archie smiled, self-assured he was physically more tested than the average citizen. Military life demanded it. A normal person, when cold, steps indoors, or when tired, goes to sleep, or when in pain, simply stops. Archie's military life was a daily ritual of suppressing those sorts of normal impulses and the result was a mental and physical toughness most would never have cause to know. He offered Merle his hand up, adding, "I've spent years of my life keeping off improvised explosives. I'll be okay here."

"Well, that's another story then. Thanks for your

service, son," Merle said accepting Archie's forearm in his grip. As Archie heaved the old mechanic to his feet, he pointed out the faded Marine Corps tattoo on the other's arm. "Right back at you, pops."

"Hoorah. So what can I do for a fellow vet?"

"I'm here to pick up my car. The mustang."

"Oh, that's you. Yeah, I don't do the paint. They hired a Mexican kid for that. He doesn't speak a lick of English but the boy can paint. Come on."

As Merle led the way through the disarray of cars in various stages of disrepair, Archie caught his foot on a power cord and upset a stack of exhausts pipes as he nearly toppled over completely. Merle paused to give him a knowing look over his shoulder before stepping out of the backdoor.

Leading Archie to a corner of the lot, he pulled a car cover from the mustang and stood back to let Archie survey the work, saying, "Kind of curious paint job. Not my sort of thing, but she looks good, I suppose."

"It was something I wanted as a younger man. In a different season of life. It was time I just did it. Now or never."

***

Archie spun the volume dial on the old car radio so he could hear the music over the wind which was washing over him through the window. He was the only vehicle on the open road and as he let his left hand ride the thermals outside the car, he felt more like he was soaring than driving. He felt free. He was headed home, but was taking the longest way possible, each mile a moment of conscious happiness. There was something about being in motion that gave him peace. The past was behind him and the future didn't matter yet.

Once at the marina, he took the car cover from the trunk and paused to once again take in the new paint job. It was Olympic blue, and instead of the usual flames coming off the front fenders, Archie had ordered yellow

wings air brushed on either side. To complete the motif,

he had painted above the driver's door, *PEGASUS*, a

name which aptly described the feeling of flight he had

while driving it. He sighed, and like a masochist, he

covered the car with the cover and walked away,

knowing that unless a medical miracle occurred, he

would probably never drive his chariot again.

CHAPTER SIXTEEN

Archie gathered tools from the holds of the Argo, preparing to occupy his mind from dark thoughts, but it was a battle he was losing as he contemplated the meaning of the dream from the night before.

He had seen himself as a Greek soldier crouching on a mountain of rubble and trapped on all sides by the encroaching flames which ravaged the city of Smyrna in 1922. He clutched the rifle the dream placed in his hands, and tilted his head towards the heavens as the flames swallowed him.

Then it was 1896 and he was a Cretan Revolutionary trapped on a mountain peak by Turkish warriors who scaled the rocks with knives in their teeth. He loaded a pistol before tucking it into the red sash around his waist and unsheathing a cutlass. He glared up at the heavy clouds above him and breathed deep as the Turkish warriors made the summit, carrying death.

480 B.C. and he was the last Spartan waiting on a sheer cliff for the Persian fighters who closed in on him from both sides like two unstoppable waves of water. He knelt, but only to scrap his heavy shield off the ground, before returning to his tired feet. He gripped the thick spear in his hand as he gazed through the slits of his bronze helmet at the heavens above, unperturbed by the rapidly advancing Persians rushing his demise.

1200 B.C. and he limped to the top of a sand dune as Achaeans and Trojans waged war behind him. He collapsed on the soft summit and pulled his helmet off, dropping it in the sand where it rolled down the dune and past his foot and the arrow lodged there. It followed the trickle of blood that poured from his heel, returning to the battle for which it had been forged.

Below him he saw a fortified encampment along the shores where the ancient trirams were beached. He knew the ship nearest him was his, for the large eye painted on the prow seemed to stare into him, imploring him to board her and sail home, but he knew it was too late as he looked over the vast ocean and raised his head to the dazzling bright sun.

That was where he woke, the sun playing on his face, beaming unusually bright through the Argo's portholes. It bothered him that even in his sleep and in the dark recesses of his brain, he knew he was going to die and was looking for the fortitude to do so bravely.

He was already at work on his vessel by the time Meaghan arrived, carefully balancing a coffee in each hand as she descended the short ramp to the dock. Archie had his back to her as she approached, crouched as he was in a dingy tied to the bow of the Argo and consumed in painting a large, simple eye on the hull. Meaghan was about to speak to announce herself when Archie beat her to the punch. "I thought I smelled beautiful," he called without turning.

"Oh boy. I brought you caffeine," she said, crouching at the edge of the dock to pass Archie the beverages.

"Coffee and beautiful women. The two things that keep me up at night," Archie quipped as he settled the drinks on the floor of the dinghy and offered Meaghan his hand, inviting her beside him.

"You and your smooth lines."

"Truthfully, I came up with that one years ago."

"I figured it was a canned one," she said squeezing next to him.

"Yeah. When I first thought it up, I said to myself 'Save this one until you find the perfect woman' and I just realized that's you."

She wanted to kiss him in that moment, but resisted the urge as she hid a pleased smile behind her coffee.

"It took you long enough."

Archie bit his cheek and chuckled, resuming his task with paint and brush.

Meaghan scrutinized his handiwork. "It's an eye, right?"

Archie nodded. It was in the fashion of those the ancient Greeks painted near the prow of their ships of war. It was a common symbol in Mediterranean culture, often referred to as an Evil Eye, which Archie considered a bit of a misnomer, for it was there to counter evil, by staring boldly back in its face. As Archie explained this to Meaghan, she nodded in half understanding then asked, "But why are you putting one on the Argo?"

"I don't know." Archie scratched his head before continuing. He hadn't really thought it out that far. "Just had a weird dream last night, I guess."

"You sailing to Troy, Archie?" Meaghan queried. She was skilled at interpreting dreams and this one made sense to her. The human brain came with its own subconscious therapist which went to work at night, analyzing and trying to solve the problems of the consciousness. Archie was in uncharted waters, his health a murky and dangerous abyss.

Archie flinched at her accidental directness. She may have been trying to use a metaphor, but yes, that was exactly how he was beginning to feel, as though each day was another step in a journey which was bringing him closer to his destiny…a destiny of doom. He would face this destiny, and while he was grateful to have Meaghan near, there was a part of him that would rather face it alone, like the men he was in his sleep, than risk her as a casualty of collateral damage.

"You know, we have to be real here. If I don't make it, I want you to be okay."

"Don't even say that."

"I've got to, Meg." The serious look in Archie's

eye piqued Meaghan. He always had a wisecrack at the ready to refuse the serious topics she offered, such was the nature of their relationship. She would be damned if she was going to indulge him now, when he wanted to voice sentiments of defeatism.

She threw her hands up in exasperation. "You're always telling me not to think negatively. What is it you say about fighting? Prepare for victory, don't ready for defeat. And now here you are getting ready to die."

"Well, I also say there is no such thing as being ready for a fight. Every fight I've ever had, when the moment came to step in the cage, I wasn't ready. There was always something more I could have done. Practiced another move or did some more cardio. Hit the bag some more. Then the cage door closes and there's no more getting ready. I'm starting to see this the same. In some quiet way, I've been getting ready to die my whole life, but that won't help me when the moment arrives."

"I don't want to hear any of this."

Archie persisted, taking her hand. "You're such a beautiful girl, Meaghan. Inside and out. And that makes me worry about you."

"Archie!"

"You're a great person, Meg. And as many people will love for you for that as will hate you for it. You're literally attractive. That means you'll attract good and bad people alike. You'll need to be careful, okay?"

Meaghan tossed his hand aside and rose quickly, almost tipping the dinghy. Archie grabbed the sides to stabilize it as she hastily stepped out and onto the dock. She turned to look down at him. "No, I don't, because I'm going to have you to look out for me."

Archie sighed, the painful sigh of a one who wished to say more than mortality could permit, communicate in ways a being could not.

She planted herself on the nearby dock box, anxiously watching the ocean, the sky, anything but Archie who had climbed out of the dinghy and was sitting beside her now.

"Hey," he whispered in her ear. She ignored him as though he hadn't spoken at all. "Meaghan," he attempted once more, in vain. Recognizing the futility, he grabbed her under the knees and hips and pulled her towards him, half onto his lap and turning her so she had to face him. She struggled a moment against him, angry tears in her eyes.

Archie shifted his weight to reach inside his pocket and pull from it a necklace with a colorful amulet swinging from the end, upon it an evil eye symbol which was similar to the one now emblazoned upon the Argo. He had retrieved it from his cherished belongings to use it as a model for the earlier artwork, but now had a better use for it. He offered it to Meaghan. "I want you to have this, Meaghan. It was my mother's. She believed one of the worst things you can feel for someone is envy, because then you send negative energy their way. She thought this protected her."

"I don't want it."

"Take it. Maybe it's just old country superstition, but at the very least it's something you can remember me by."

Meaghan pushed it away and crossed her arms in insubordination. She turned her nose up at his outstretched hand. "Seven."

"Huh?"

"That's my ring size and that's the only jewelry you are going to give me."

His eyes widened softly and he smirked sheepishly, becoming aware that if he asked her to marry him, she'd say yes. Meaghan's resolute visage seemed to correct him. "No, Arch. I'd say *definitely*." It was a query he might pose if only he was in control of his destiny, for as it was, he could better promise to make her a widow than a wife. He pocketed the necklace, disappointed that it was refused but appreciating the kind of wit and stubbornness he had encountered. "Okay, but you are going to have to do the proposing."

"Oh, you think so?"

"Yeah, I'm a progressive man. You'll have to wear a woman tuxedo though. And I want it to be special, of course. Like on a hot air balloon or surrounded by wild horses...but I still want to be surprised, you know?"

"You're ridiculous. Always trying to get me on my knees."

Archie chucked briefly, pulling Meaghan entirely onto his lap. She laughed, mostly from relief at the pleasant turn in conversation until she noticed the serious look return in his eyes.

"What?"

Archie shrugged. "Eh…I've just always had this sort of conflict in me. This struggle between wanting to be free and wanting to be close to someone."

"Why can't you do both?"

"I never do anything half way. Whatever I do, I do it with everything that I am. There is nothing left for anything else."

"I don't need a lot of love, Archie."

"But you deserve it. After I lost Diane, I felt the issue was more or less settled for me. You've been changing my thinking again. Well that, and I admit, the unwelcome addition to my frontal lobe."

Meaghan placed a small hand over Archie's built chest which had he had constructed through years of pushups, pushing against the Earth to mount a wall of fleshy armor around his most vital organ. "Archie, you have such a big heart I don't think you need to love me with everything. Just you loving me a little, is more than enough."

"You think so?"

"I do. I love you and I don't want to lose you."

"I know the feeling, kid."

Archie cast a long look at the setting sun. This illness was the first sabbatical from war and strife he had known. The cancer was almost a lesser burden than daily combat, an ironic reprieve. In lieu of fighting, he was given nothing else to do but think. There was a time he thought little of life itself. The actual act of living was only a means to an end, to honor and legacy which held more value than the lives he took or even his own which he risked. Now he saw that he might find more meaning not in the accumulated sum, but in the sole and present moment of life. He held Meaghan tighter, allowing his feelings free reign to attach to her. He, who never stopped fighting, had finally surrendered.

CHAPTER SEVENTEEN

Archie reclined in a soft chair as one of several patients in the ward receiving chemotherapy. He felt sick, feeling the life giving blood which left him via the tube in his arm return with the chemical concoction added. Instinctively, he wanted to yank the tube from his arm for the idea of some foreign substance entering his veins was abhorrent. He knew it was medicine but couldn't help cringing as though it was laundry detergent or motor oil coming through the line. That the history of the treatment had origins as a derivative of the mustard gas used in the First World War did little to assuage this sentiment. The chemical cocktail often caused symptoms worse than the cancer itself. It was as though an evil spirit had entered his body, and the only way to exorcise it was for a priest to make his being intolerable to inhabit, scalding it with Holy Water. Cavanaugh was his priest, the chemo his acidic water and the cancer his demon. Whoever could hold out longer would possess the body.

The television mounted in the corner of the room served a purpose similar to the white plastic cones dogs wore post op to keep them from gnawing at their wounds, curbing his inclination to pull free from the siphon. As he watched the black and white rendition of *Frankenstein* Meaghan sat beside him, as absorbed in watching him as he appeared to be in the out of date film. She was thinking about the events of that morning.

The soothing swaying of the Argo had put her into a sleep so deep she slept later than normal, precariously close to the start of her first class of the day. Archie insisted on making her breakfast to go, arguing less than eloquently that her, "liberal fucking professors could fuck themselves, she wasn't going hungry." She was aware that a man who had so often faced death, deemed every other consequence so trivial that an admonishment from an academic was laughable. She worked around him, grabbing her things and paying little attention to him as he swore and grumbled in an exchange he was apparently having with the news anchor broadcasting over the radio. She tuned it out automatically after the first few words for she had gathered enough. More violence in Iraq, more killed, et cetera. It was the mantra of the past decade and as daily as the weather. Being younger than Archie, there was no time in her life when she could recall a world in which her country was not at war. In her haste, she had failed to notice that Archie seemed more personally invested in the transmission.

It wasn't until she approached the electronic swinging barricade that admitted entry to her campus garage that she realized she had left her purse containing her parking pass on the Argo. She thought to text Archie a request to bring it to her, but then remembered he wasn't supposed to be behind the wheel. So she dismissed the text all together, racing back to the Argo.

When she rushed aboard, Archie was sitting in the cabin, tying the laces of his combat boots. The very same boots, she conjectured, he wore in Iraq. He was in his complete uniform, the beige and tan desert pattern the troops had worn only early on in the war.

"Arch?" She questioned.

He looked at her, trying desperately to hide that he had been on the verge of tears.

"I was just trying it on, wondering if it still fit."

"It's okay."

The radio broadcast earlier had set him off. Another report of the growing insurgent group in Iraq, terrorizing the people he had fought for. Now they had spread and were defacing Europe. To the world, this was a new, difficult to understand adversary but for him it was an old acquaintance, an enemy he had known with the closeness of a childhood friend. He tried to forget them, to make believe he'd never see them again, but here they were once more, coming for him and everything he stood for. On a tactical level, this was an easy enemy to defeat, but strategically, they were formidable in that they understood well the Western world which could not comprehend them.

He had often felt that he was fighting on two fronts when he faced this enemy, placed between them and his superiors who were incompetent, blinded by their ambitions. For them, doing the right thing had become whatever led to the next promotion. He didn't need bars on his collar to tell him what was right, nor did he suppose that God cared what rank he was.

They were not leaders, but politicians and in the most charitable use of the word. He grew sick at heart, watching them enable these killers to escape, mock America, murder civilians, kill his comrades and wreak havoc. As they were today.

He knew well the moment he decided to leave the military, realizing that he could never defeat this enemy with the leadership installed. A new troop rotation had arrived, more lamb for the slaughter. His boots and uniform were as worn and faded as his smile, while theirs were bright and excited, like kids on the first day of school with squeaky new sneakers and book bags. He watched over them, like a concerned grandparent, knowing the harsh reality that awaited them.

Western civilization was now in the same predicament, even though this was not the first evil to have threatened it, the Nazis having been only stories by the time he was born. It was an evil his Poupou vanquished, but when he heard of them, he could not imagine being able bodied and alive and not doing something to stop them. Now they were a reality. In fact, it was worse than that, for the true extent of Third

Reich's atrocities was not even known until after the invasion. Instead, he was already aware that seven year old girls were being kidnaped, raped and fed to their parents and still his country was hesitant to put boots on the ground, because they were scared. He was too. He wore those boots once and there was nothing to show for it, besides bent and broken feet for him and that living hell in Iraq now threatening the West. This was worst part of being a veteran. Able to place bullets into the heartless chests of these evil men, but too far removed from the conflict to do so.

The fatigues called to him often from the hold where he placed them when he first moved aboard, but never disturbed them, perturbed by the peculiar notion that if he wore the uniform again, he'd die in it. Literally perhaps, but also the version of him that life had intended would have perished entirely. When he opened the hatch that morning, no longer able to resist the curious summons, the moths that swarmed around his face stung him with the poisonous recollections of war, death, sadness and misery.

It wasn't that he regretted leaving the military, only that his reasons for joining had not likewise abandoned him. And yet another enlistment would have consumed him easily, for he was already partly digested.

As Archie rose, Meaghan saw him more clearly than she ever had before. His past was ever present. Behind his bravado, his feelings ran deep as the fathomless sea, crushing him the deeper he dove. He started to say something to dismiss himself, but it came out strange and was ended prematurely by Meaghan throwing her arms around him, not wanting to see him suffer another vulnerable moment in the fabric which so obviously haunted him.

As she clutched his hand, the one not fixed to the transfusion, it dawned on her that the wars fought abroad had finally hit home for her.

"Thank you for doing this, Archie. I know you didn't want to."

Archie broke away from the film to shake his head and kiss her hand. "No, but I want you."

"I just want you to get better."

"As my Iraqi brothers used to say, 'Inshah Allah'...God willing."

Meaghan studied Archie. It was not unusual for him to make such statements regarding the divine. He was sure of himself and it showed when he spoke of the spiritual. There was never any doubt in his voice and it was so casual and natural, odd in a time when it wasn't particularly trendy to discuss such beliefs. Far better to admit some restrained version of faith only when directly pressed, yet Archie didn't feel the need to separate his beliefs from his logic. She squeezed his hand. "I wish I had the faith you have sometimes. I've never seen God, or Allah, or really felt any super natural force."

"Well, how many shooting stars have you seen in your life?" Archie countered.

"I think I've seen one or two. Why, how many have you seen?"

"Too many to count. Hundreds probably…hell, maybe thousands."

"No way! How is that possible?"

"One day I stopped looking down and started looking up. You have to change perspective if you ever want to see some things."

"So you've seen God? When?" Meaghan pressed, expecting Archie to back pedal in some manner. To her surprise, he answered, "When I was stationed in Alaska, I used to go hiking by myself. You're not really supposed to do that."

"That sounds like your modus operandi."

Archie smirked briefly, but his eyes glazed over as he recalled the day, so many years before. He saw himself there, on that treacherous icy pass and continued, "I got myself stranded on this peak during a blizzard. It just came out of nowhere…the temperature dropped forty degrees in less than a minute. I had to take my gloves off to fix my ice cleats, which was a mistake because I couldn't get them warm again."

Archie recalled hunkering behind a large rock, desperately trying to warm his hands by placing them inside his jacket and blowing hot air into his gloves. "Then the sun dropped and it got even colder. It got so bad, I wasn't even worried about losing my hands anymore. I didn't think I was going to make it down alive at all. Hell, no one even knew I was out there."

It was then he lost his footing and slipped down the mountain, scrambling desperately for a hold. He came to a hard landing only a few feet from a sheer drop into an abyss, trembling equally with fear and cold.

"I could barely move. Truth be told, I was scared to move. I thought my next step would be my last. So I prayed. I prayed to God to save me."

A white object zoomed just inches from Archie's head, so fast its shape was merely a blur. He scanned the sky after it passed and found it there, fluttering above. "It was a dove."

The small bird circled Archie in the swirling winter snow and he rose, seemingly oblivious to the violent storm which raged around him. "There are no doves in Alaska, let alone at that altitude or in those conditions. But I know what I saw. And in that moment, I knew I was going to be okay."

He clutched Meaghan's hand and looked her steadfast in the eye. "When the impossible becomes possible…that's the face of God, Meg."

There were times science admitted defeat but

faithfully argued the day would come when it had advanced far enough to offer explanations for the unexplained…yet there were other times an event flew in the face of established science. A thing which could not happen…somehow happened. These were miracles and Archie was well aware that he was in desperate need of one now.

It was early evening when they returned to the waiting Argo, but it felt much later to Archie who was already feeling the effects of the chemotherapy. They had stopped off for a meal at a diner on the way home, but had to ask for the check prematurely as he started to crash, losing his appetite as a heavy nausea settled in. Meaghan gingerly eased him into bed, Archie sighing and grunting with the effort while Olive danced on the blanket sniffing his face with a wet nose.

Archie pulled the covers to his chin as Meaghan opened the hatch above the berth before lying next to him. Meaghan gazed at him while he looked out at the stars which seemed so heavy and close that the sky felt like a ceiling he might have been able to touch.

"What are you thinking about?" she pondered aloud, not meaning to actually speak the words. It was a question she often had while in his presence, but this time it voiced itself without her permission.

Archie answered, "Frankenstein...the movie, from earlier. You know that book was written by a teenage girl?"

"Yes, I've heard that. But you know, that was like two hundred years ago. The average life expectancy was probably thirty so people did things when they were a lot younger."

"Nah, I know, but that's the thing. How did she know that electricity would bring him to life? Sure, we use defibrillators now, but back then...unless..."

"Unless what?

"Maybe that's just one of those things we've always known as human beings, even before we could explain or see it."

Archie held his hand in the air above them, grasping it open and closed repeatedly against the starry night sky. "If you could see electricity, you'd see it coursing through my hand right now, pulsing every time I open and close it." Archie tapped his chest…his heart. "And it all comes from this thing."

"You have the mind of a scientist, you know that?"

"Scientists..." Archie scoffed. "They know the body is made of energy, atoms really. But they refuse to call it what it is…soul. And because they won't call it that they don't know where it comes from or where it goes when we die either...only they admit it has to go somewhere."

Meaghan sat up on her elbow to look Archie in

the eye. "And where does the mighty Archie reason it to go?"

"Yes, I am mighty. Thank you for acknowledging that. And I think it depends. If you were a negative person who said and did negative things, it stands to reason your energy would go someplace negative."

"Hell," Meaghan surmised.

"And if you were generally a positive person, your soul ought to go someplace positive."

"Heaven."

"When you put it that way, it's pretty crazy to think they nailed a guy to a cross for saying that, huh?"

Meaghan sighed, "It's crazy they ever nailed anyone to a cross for anything."

They lay quiet for a pause, but Archie had an idea of the topic of which she ruminated in the silence.

He knew she was trying to reconcile the

misdeeds of ancient religions with what she felt to be intuitively so. The denominations of man had at times alienated those seeking spirituality through oppressive intolerance, even violence. These institutions had attempted the impossible in trying to quantify the divine and tame man when neither was achievable. So many denounced religion and the spiritual awareness that went with it, seeking their answers in the material world of science. Yet science without spirit was simply another dogma, but few were repulsed from it when it created gun powder, the atomic bomb or categorized race. It was no trouble for Archie to see that the common denominator in both cases was man. The atmosphere contained twenty-one percent oxygen and he did not suppose it a coincidence that humans required only sixteen percent to breath and fire exactly the same to combust. These were the only three agents required to burn the world, anything else was superfluous.

He heard once that scientists knew more about outer space than the bottom of the ocean. So too did he believe the world had neglected a subject much closer to home for loftier pursuits. The very soul was ignored.

Spirituality was, he contended, as important as mathematics, physics, and chemistry. The forms of communication which once bound all living beings as one, even before the advent of language, were replaced by the radio, telephone and finally, the internet. The part of the human brain which once sent and received these messages had atrophied, leaving the soul both deaf and mute within the creatural carcass.

He knew religious strife had caused crusades which many could not forgive, but was intimately aware that such violence paled in scope to the wars and genocides perpetrated by governments and political ideologies. Still, he heard few call for the limits on government power that had long since restricted religion to its proper place. Sure, most conceded that government was not a perfect institution, but they recognized it was better than no governance at all. Why, he wondered, was not the same logic applied to religion, which despite its failures, had preserved some of the last secrets of the divine through the bloody ages. While government was the search for an ideal way of occupying the Earth, religion was the pursuit of the soul to inhabit the body. Neither had achieved perfection but were either of them worthy of being forsaken entirely?

Even as he was allowing medical science an attempt to save his life, he had not relinquished his belief in the power of the spirit to heal the body. Surely it was possible, for it was undeniable that flesh corrupted spirit. Why should it not work the other way around?

She broke the silence. "What do you think Heaven is like, Archie?"

"I don't know. Maybe it's whatever you want it

to be? I mean, if you spend every day of your life, thinking, believing in one thing, it's bound to come true, right? I gotta make myself believe I'm going to win the fight to get in that cage. If I don't believe, chances are, not only won't I win, I probably wouldn't even get in there in the first place."

"What would you want it to be like?"

"I'd want to see everyone again. People who have passed, you know? I want to see my Popou again." He didn't have to explain this Greek word for grandfather to Meaghan. She had heard it before and noticed his genuine reverence for his elder generation as a trait which distinguished him as a Greek American, for the magnitude to which he not just loved, but respected his grandfather, seemed less characteristic of American culture than Greek.

Archie scratched Olive's head which she had settled on his chest. "And my old bulldog from when I was a kid. We called him Chopper. I loved that dog and he loved me. He died the day I shipped out for boot camp." Archie kept the memory of that dog so dear and vivid that it felt like his totem at times, reminding him to be tough, stubborn and loyal. Dying when he did made the point of his life clear to Archie. The dog served as a childhood friend and his life ended the day Archie ceased to be a boy and became a soldier.

He rolled over sleepily, pulling one of Meaghan's arms over him as he closed his eyes. "And I don't want there to be any talking. I want us all to just know each other, to just understand one another entirely and perfectly. Best part is, we'd be free of these damn bodies. Wouldn't have to worry about working and paying bills just to keep from starving or suffering. This body was made to make us suffer..."

***

Meaghan, already fresh and dressed for the day,

leaned into the cabin to check on Archie who peered painfully from under the blanket. He had woken up before her but had not budged an inch. He was imagining the cancer cells within him scurrying like cockroaches through a house just fumigated.

"How do you feel?" she whispered.

Archie groaned. "You know how a cat plays with a mouse before killing it? I feel like life is doing that with me."

"I should cut class today, stay with you," Meaghan doted, feeling his forehead maternally an instant before realizing the motion was useless. The man she loved had cancer, not the flu.

"Nah, Meg, I don't think I can perform to my usual mind blowing standards."

"Shoot. Maybe I'll stay at my place tonight then and get some studying in."

"Yeah, you might want to…at least you'll be

getting something in. It's my own fault. I set the bar too high," Archie said, exaggerating the strain in his voice as he curled the blankets around him.

Meaghan leaned over to kiss him very lightly on the forehead, careful not to jar or disturb him. As she moved away, Archie snatched her by her shirt collar for a full kiss on the mouth.

"You're incorrigible." Meaghan breathed as she pulled away.

Wincing as he slid out of bed he said, "I have my moments."

"And your limits. You should sleep in, Soldier."

Archie ignored her and stepped out of bed, clutching the boat walls for support when surprised to find how debilitatingly sore he was. He cursed himself inwardly for being taken aback when the doctor had warned him this was a probable side effect of the chemo which attacked dividing cells…cancerous and healthy alike. The soreness Archie felt now emanated in his bones, where the marrow was being destroyed. He examined his face and physique in the mirror above the head, dismayed to find he looked like hell. His skin was dull and sunken under the eyes, as though he hadn't slept for a month. "God. This ain't fair. I've spent years eating right and working out. And for what? This is destroying my body!"

"Archie, don't do that to yourself," Meaghan urged from the galley where she was counting out the various pills Archie had been prescribed.

"It's true though. I've practiced fitness like the ancient Greeks did, putting it on par with my education. You know, this country is unhealthy because we've forgotten that. There's no such thing as physical education in schools. It's just fuck'n dodge ball and grab ass! So dumb kids become fat adults and no one knows why. And then every other commercial these days is some crazy weight loss pill or hopeless workout. The Greeks used to say exercise is to the body as music is to the soul. That's why you have all this garbage music now with no soul, because no one can do a damn sit-up anymore!" Archie was ranting, despite discovering soreness deep in his throat.

Meaghan looked him over a brief moment, nodding and trying to take him seriously but failing and bursting into a fit of laughter.

Archie was wounded by her amusement. "Oh, so America is fat and I'm sick and you think this is all funny?"

Meaghan came close, tittering still but apologetic in her embrace. "I've never seen you sick before. You're so grumpy and it's adorable."

Getting the joke, Archie chuckled at himself and pinched her lightly. "Now I just wish cancer was contagious."

Meaghan squirmed playfully away to retrieve the pills she had counted.

Archie sighed, "Truthfully, I sort of knew this day would come, when I'd have to let go of my body a tad. Just didn't expect it so soon is all."

"What are you talking about now?" Meaghan asked as she filled a glass with water while Archie flexed and continued his self-examination.

"I mean, you have to let go of some things. Jesus had to sacrifice His body to ascend and in a pretty brutal way at that. Gandhi too. That guy took some beatings that made my worst cage fight look like a hugging contest! He starved himself almost to death to free his people. He couldn't have done any of that if he cared about his flesh more than his cause."

Meaghan gave Archie the water with another cup full of pills. "But you just have to get well, Soldier. That's it. You can put fighting for your causes on hold.

You're not Gandhi."

"I know. I'm not half the man he was," Archie said, quite seriously. He thought much of himself but knew his limits. He could take a beating but to watch people he cared about abused by bullies and not retaliate with his full force…this he knew he could never do.

***

Archie followed Meaghan onto the deck of the Argo, wearing the blanket like a cape. As they settled onto the fiberglass bench, it was Meaghan who watched the sun finishing its climb and Archie who watched her. When she noticed his steady gaze, she touched her face self-consciously. "Did I mess my make up?"

Archie shook his head, despite the vertigo the slight movement caused him. "It's just a shame you can't see yourself through my eyes."

"Oh? And what would I see if I could?"

"You'd see a girl who is beautiful in a way you

forgot existed."

"I like where this is going. Sir, you may continue to elaborate on my beauty," Meaghan played along.

"You remind me of how I used to look at women, before hormones kicked in and sex entered the picture. Like when I was a small boy and I'd see a stunning woman and all I could say or even think was, wow. Pure wow."

Meaghan leaned onto Archie's chest as he wrapped the blanket around her. "I like you on chemo...you're soft."

"Well, don't get used to it. Once I get better..."

"Yeah?"

"You're gonna get it."

"Promises, promises. I have to do a quick shift after classes, but I'll see you tonight?"

"Yeah, of course. Here, let me walk you to your

car," Archie offered, rising painfully. Meaghan opened her mouth to protest but Archie shrugged her off. "It will be good for me. If you want, I'll give you a quick tutorial on how to drive?"

"I know how to drive, Archie."

"That's debatable."

CHAPTER NINETEEN

Archie stood upright and strong, returning Meaghan's wave when she drove past. As soon as she was out of sight he keeled over at the waist and vomited violently. Olive scampered to inspect the regurgitated mess, honing in with her nose close to the ground. Archie groaned and shooed her away. "No girl, its *skata*," he admonished using the Greek word for "shit."

Normally he started his day with three raw eggs mixed in a glass of whole milk, a simple recipe that provided him with the proteins and nutrients he needed without consideration for a lavish appetite or delicate palate. However, the agitation the chemotherapy stirred within his bowels demanded he forgo his Spartan diet altogether. Instead of breakfast, he took up a game of darts underneath the overhang, almost amused by how poor of a throw he had now as a result of the treatment. For every set he tossed, at least one dart missed the board altogether, while the other two failed to bridge the distance at all, clattering to the dock. He was almost amused by the unusual heft of the dainty darts in his normally strong grip.

Archie was stooping to collect the projectiles when the sound of a car driving way too fast put him on guard. He recognized Mackey's truck, and for a moment thought the other was horsing around but when he saw the look in Mackey's eyes the hair sprung up on his neck. It was a look he knew from when the spared returned from war and could not speak the names of the departed with voice, resorting instead to a stare filled with tears. Nothing said more than a tear and Archie understood that which glossed over Mackey's eyes now and dulled the otherwise piercing green of his eyes…this tear whispered, "Byron."

CHAPTER TWENTY

With Mackey at his heels, Archie burst into the recovery room. Mackey ran right into the back of him when Archie slowed suddenly at the sight of his beloved friend unconscious in the hospital bed. Mackey had filled him in during the panicked race to the hospital. Byron's heart had stopped and for a time he had been clinically dead. The doctors were able to resuscitate him, though the final outcome was far from certain. Archie almost found it ironic that his friend who so loved the resurrected Jesus had been resurrected himself.

He moved close to the mattress with the intention of gripping his confidant's limp paw in his own, but the intravenous needle sticking out of the back of Byron's hand and the heart beat monitor gripping the forefinger deterred him. Instead he placed his hand on the vacillating chest. Afraid to jar the fragile form beneath his palm, he froze there, solid as an igloo stands while a hot fire burns within the icy confines. In his left ear, he heard only the beeping of electronics and the screeching cacophony of the hallway teeming with nurses and doctors yelling at each other. It was the clamor of humans fighting to put the chaos of the world in order. In his right ear he heard only the gentle, peaceful wheezing and sighing of his comrade, struggling to live as the tide fights to overtake the shore and retreats only to attempt again.

Mackey's voice broke the observant dichotomy from where he hung by the door, unable as he was to look at his badly injured friend. "It happened so fast, Archie. Before anyone could even stop it, it was already done."

Mackey recounted the violence of the night before when Bryon faced Heckman in a bout that was, as it turned out, to the death. Bryon had done well, remarkably well for a retired veteran of the cage and even more so considering his opponent. For a time it appeared Heckman had finally met his match, even once losing his footing and tumbling haphazardly to the mat. When this fall occurred, Byron stepped back and let the other rise, not willing to allow a misstep to claim his victory. When, a round later, Byron slipped on a spot slicked with the combined sweat of the two fighters, Heckman showed no such mercy. He didn't hesitate to pounce on Byron before he could recover and rain down powerful blows which pressed his knuckles through the leather of the gloves, finding stoppage on his opponent's skull. Bryon struggled heroically which prompted Heckman to rain down a series of elbows. The referee tried to stop him, seizing him by the shoulder and screaming, "No elbows, damn it!" Heckman, frenzied now by the sight of gushing blood, pushed the mediator away and continued to batter his felled opponent with the illegal maneuver. Mackey tried frantically to intervene, but his attempt to open the cage door was thwarted by Heckman's corner man who pushed him out of the way. By the time he was back on his feet and rushing the cage with the rest of Heckman's entourage, it was too late.

Archie clenched the rail of Bryon's hospital bed as Mackey continued, "He's been sleeping mostly. They have him on a lot of meds. He's got a fractured skull, and his orbital socket has been smashed to pieces. The doctors say even if they can save the eye, he'll probably never see out of it."

Archie shook his head, trying to understand. "Spike elbows aren't even legal in the UFC…and this is why. What was he thinking? He hasn't fought in years."

"He was trying to save the church, Arch. He said he fought enough fights for nothing, he didn't mind fighting one for something."

Archie whirled around, challenging Mackey in

lieu of his unconscious friend. "But of all the people to fight, Heckman? The cheating steroid junkie?"

Mackey explained placating, as though he were the accused, "Joe put it together, Archie. He knew Bryon needed the cash, and he couldn't find anyone to take Heckman on anymore." Mackey paused a moment to straighten up, remembering that he did not own the guilt he nonetheless felt. "God damn, Joe."

Archie pulled a cheaply cushioned chair underneath him as he spat, "No...I'll damn Joe."

Mackey, having no reply or the stomach to see his mangled friend, stealthily left the room. Archie however, sat staring and as a pot slowly comes to boil, so did the blood in his heart cook with a molten rage that burned his exterior into a thick, hard, crust. He was once more submerged in the hate and vitriol which he had felt only in war. It gained new breath beneath his lungs, bolstering his exhalations such that each inflation gave him the power of a dozen. The hate which he attempted to abolish from his being post war had only formed a terrible abscess, waiting to burst and burn like a thousand ulcers. It was a hemorrhaging wrath which his veins sucked up like the thirsted roots of an old tree long subjected to drought. As his fervor increased, he felt that so too did his mass. In his mounting fury he felt invincible, as though he could fell any foe with a mere two fingers. But any foe would not do. It had to be Heckman. Only Heckman's broken body could be held for recompense.

For too long Archie had allowed this nemesis to hide behind the wall of advantage the steroids afforded him, a buttress which thwarted the valiant attempts of others. But no more. Archie would finally scale that formidable palisade from which Heckman cowered while beating his own chest.

His rage was unyielding and cyclic, perpetuated

by alternating waves of guilt and anger. Guilt that he had forsaken his warrior ethos and put his own well-being above that of his comrades. He had led the fighters into the Rock's and deserted them there. Byron, compelled by his honor as good and decent men are, had no choice but to take up command in his absence. Anger, because the world around him was intolerable. He was in the grip of this mad storm when a powerful sound pulled him from it in an instant. It was the terrible groan of an ally awaking to new pain.

"Did I win?" Bryon croaked from a throat parched with thirst and dried blood. He meant it as a joke, but the battered voice guised it. Yet Archie understood, as he always did his friend, for words were mere companions to their union. When they did converse, Archie often felt as though he was speaking with his own soul.

Archie tried to laugh but the humor could not

stem the tears that fell, one from each eye for the sorrow and overwhelming relief that overtook him.

Even in his battered state, Byron tried to assure him. "Hey, I'm okay, brother. How long was I out?"

"Ten years."

"Yeah?"

"Yeah. A lot's changed. Mackey has come out of the closet and your wardrobe is back in style...only one of those things I didn't see coming."

Byron laughed but the light convulsion flexed his broken ribs and his piercing wince dismantled the brief levity they had tried to construct.

In the solemn pause that ensued, Archie pondered a question he had held since the day they met but had never asked. He looked at Byron in the hospital bed and was reminded by how their positions were reversed not so long ago. Life was a fragile thing and if Archie held the question any longer he may lose the chance to put it forward again.

"Why'd you do it, Byron? All those years ago? I've always wondered. There I was rotting in the drunk tank and you show up out of nowhere. You didn't even know me."

"Every day of my life, I ask God to use me to help someone. You needed it that day."

"For the record, Mackey started that fight. He was a real punk back then."

"You were different back then too, Arch…all wrath and anger."

***

It happened a few months after Archie had settled in North Carolina. He had yet to work out a way to keep his sailboat cool in the summer heat and was seeking midday refuge in a poorly kept bar. Moreover, he was there to continue the daily assault on his being by drinking himself into oblivion. He cursed that God had given man an anatomy which allowed him to wash blood from his hands yet left him unable to scrub the folds of the brain, rinsing it of coagulated memories. It was a grey chunk of marble which the events of life chiseled to a final form that could never be undone, the chips on the floor never restored. It seemed every day he became something less than what he could have once been.

He was gazing through the bangs of his disheveled hair which draped over his eyes like a sheen curtain, fumbling with Diane's memorial bracelet. Her death had been like the collapse of a star which formed a black hole that could only be witnessed by the bending light around it, so strong was its pull that not even a photon could escape. Archie was that bent light, and a look into his eyes bespoke her presence to those who could not otherwise know she had existed.

While the bar saved him from the assault of the sun, it invited an attack by the demon of war who was lancing Archie's conscious with painful aberrations. The memories spawned from his brain as vile snakes, boring through his skull to hiss immutably next to his ears. He would see them hanging from his scalp whenever he looked in the rearview mirror of his past, begging him to slay them.

When the television above the dusty bottles broadcasted political anchors debating the merit of the Iraq war, Archie was quick to order, "Whisky, and shut that fuckin' thing off." But the damage had been done, the slithering serpents falling down to his neck.

He gave up on politics when he abandoned nationalism, an idea that the accomplishments of some were shared by all. In fact it was the concept itself which had first deserted him, for it hurt to invest so much for the ideals of his nation just to watch them trampled on by his own countrymen. He tired of clinging to it while the apathetic strolled across his back. Amoral politicians sold his freedoms away while he offered a sacrifice of his own blood and flesh to preserve them. Moreover, he felt as though he alone lay awake in a dark room full of sleeping people. It was time to wake up and turn on the lights, but whenever he tried the people would turn from their slumber to chastise him, demanding he tiptoe in the dark and not stir them for they preferred to be asleep while he could not help but be awake. To love his country now meant bearing a broken heart, so he strived towards deliberate apathy instead, as though he was getting over an unrequited love.

Archie shot back another swig and shook his head, the toxic swill swishing in his mouth like the ocean of emotion in his heart whenever he heard this same old sentiment about Iraq and oil. It bothered him because he knew there was truth to it. There would always be the reason for war, and then there would be the motivations. War needed a pretty face. The Greek generals gave the theft of awe inspiring Helen as their reason for war against the Trojans, but certainly they were motivated by what the capture of the Trojan city would mean to Greek economy. For whoever possessed that walled city also controlled the trade between the Aegean and the Black Sea and subsequently commanded the imports of bronze. Controlling this precious metal in the Bronze Age was not so dissimilar to controlling oil in the modern one. And yet that was not what the heroes on both sides fought for, or died for.

Certainly, he did not fight for some crude substance, but rather the loftier ideals of honor, duty and freedom. This is what had propelled him initially, a crusade to restore breath taking Lady Liberty to her rightful throne, though now he was finding it difficult to reconcile the result, for after fighting so he felt entitled to no honor or any duty to wage war for others. Nor was there any freedom for one who lacked peace of mind. He would have preferred to live with total pride or absolute regret than a confusing mixture of both on the same subject. The whisky turned bitter and thick in his mouth, for in his mind it had turned to that slick, black, crude and still, he could not, would not accept that what Diane died for was not in fact what she fought for.

He toyed now with the idea of anarchy, not in the hellish, chaotic sense, but simply one where there was no government capable of amassing an army. For wars were fought by armies belonging to countries run by governments. Therefore, he reasoned cheerlessly, there could be no war without a nation.

So deep was he brooding that he almost didn't notice when three young guys came into the bar, screeching the toes of the stools they pulled back to plop down directly next to him. *Only a civilian*, he thought grumpily, would sit so close to a total stranger in an otherwise empty bar.

The bartender nodded their way and called to the one nearest Archie, "The usual, Mackey?"

"You talked me into it, Ziggy," Mackey quipped as he reached familiarly over the bar to retrieve the television remote, powering it back on. While Mackey turned his attention to scouring the outdated set for something of interest, Archie returned once more to his drunken reverie. He was yanked once out of his daze by Mackey shouting, "Oh shit, McLaren is fighting Rodriguez tonight!"

Archie glanced at the screen mounted above the bar to see that Mackey had settled on an Ultimate Fighting Match. He grimaced and swallowed half his stiff drink in an effort to leave sooner rather than later.

Suddenly Mackey jumped from his stool, slapping the bar while shouting, "Boom, baby!" in response to the exciting turn of events in the televised match. Archie winced when the palm struck the bar, which in his ears alone resounded like a near explosion accompanied by the yelling of comrades, crackling of a radio and ensuing bursts of machine gun fire. When the phantom noise abated, he glared at Mackey who was elbowing his companions and shouting, "Geez Louis that was fast!"

"Settle down, Thelma," Archie growled, rumbling like an old soul threatening to escape a young body.

Mackey turned to confront Archie who didn't look up from his drink. "Are you talking to me? You got a problem, buddy?"

"None you want to be a part of."

"That right, tough guy? You don't like sports?"

"Sports are the opium of the masses," Archie sneered, unable to tolerate the passion men showed for a game but lacked towards the deeper subjects of life. He could not get excited about an inconsequential contest after participating in mortal competition on the battlefield.

Clearly confused by the reply, Mackey looked over his shoulder at his two friends, encouraged by their presence. Deciding to act tough he replied, "Maybe there's a soap opera on for you."

At this, Archie finally turned from his glass to level his gaze on Mackey, sizing the other only by the eyes while Mackey looked him over entirely. They were two kinds of tough guys. Mackey, emboldened by a surety of his abilities to inflict injury, and Archie, equally sure there was no injury that he could not endure, none that could defeat him, for the one he carried inside was a torment without compare.

They slowly pushed their chairs out from the bar like a ritual preceding a gunfight in the old west as Mackey and his cohorts formed a ring around him, Archie clenched his fists and felt thankful to finally have someone to fight…

***

Archie wasn't released from the county jail until well into the next day when he was finally sober enough to blow a negative reading into the police station's breathalyzer. It was a matter of policy that those released be fully cognitive. Ironic as it was, Archie's current policy was to be anything but. A buzzer sounded as he shoved aside the heavy steel door, squinting painfully through one bruised eye at the sun's rays which pierced him like arrows from a deliberate bow. He regretted his reflective grimace which caused the congealed blood on his split lip to crack.

It had been so long since he had been sober that he moved stiffly and awkwardly now without the drunken swagger, like a sailor returning to land. Finding it exhausting, he took a seat on a steel bench and leaned his back against the metal fencing which pressed small squares into his skin and revitalized him like ghetto acupuncture. He gave no attention to the man on the other side of the bench who was paying Archie a great deal of it through surreptitious sideways glances.

Digging into the paper bag the guard had given him on his way out, Archie found his wallet and broken phone, smashed to worthlessness during his bout at the bar. He smiled sadly that both items now contained the same worth. He was literally broke. Life was kicking him in the teeth so often he only had mealy gums with which to bite back, to defend himself. He had been losing at every turn and starving for a win, but now he was completely defunct. He didn't know what his next move was or why he should get off the bench. It was worse than indecision, which implied a set of choices. He felt he had none at all as he reached into the bag for the last item which he clamped on its usual place on his wrist.

The man on the bench held a cigarette to Archie, snapping him out of his despair so he could shake his head in refusal of the offer.

"You look like hell," Bryon said as he lit his own smoke.

"You should see the other three guys," Archie grumbled.

"I did. I'm a friend of theirs."

Archie pivoted on the bench to look Bryon full on. He had been scheduled to stay in jail for a week and half to attend his arraignment, unless he could post bail, which he couldn't. So it was quite the surprise when they released him stating his, "friend" posted bail for him.

"You're the guy that bailed me out, aren't you?"

"Byron," he said, offering his hand.

"Achilles."

"You serious?"

"It's a family name...but my friends call me, Archie."

***

Byron's voice was little more than a wheeze as he struggled against his bruised trachea. "The way they spoke of you...how you fought. There was a look in their eyes, like they saw something that moved them. I wanted to see it too."

Archie nodded, recalling those dark days which seemed as though a former self suffered in a past life. "When I came back from Afghanistan, I wasn't sure what hurt worse...the things I lost or the things I picked up. I was so sick of losing at life. You put me in that cage, the one place victory couldn't run from me and you gave me something to fight for. You saved my life, Byron."

"You saved mine, Archie. I was as lost as you, training any jerk for a bit of money. That was wrong. I found my calling in life because of you."

Inside, Archie wept, knowing how close the two friends came to going their whole lives saying everything dear to their hearts and yet never voicing this truth, that between them existed a force which propelled them both to greater destinies.

"What's your calling, Byron?"

"To find guys like you used to be. Good men in bad places, and teach them to fight. From the inside out."

Archie smiled, but inside he was still running hot…he felt like a bad man in a bad place. His heart was pierced, cleaved in two and like an atom split, the nuclear eruption would be all consuming.

CHAPTER TWENTY-ONE

Archie gripped the wheel of the Pegasus in hands made tight by rage. He left the military, gave up on war but war had come to him. He yearned to learn a life of love and peace, but he had discovered the folly of it instead. *Do not confuse love with peace. The greatest cause for war God has ever given, is love. There is no compassion in allowing bad men free reign, ignorance to abound or illusions to stand. Bad men must be muzzled, ignorance abolished and illusions shattered.* That was love and it was the force that drove him now with the same dominant intensity with which he steered the Pegasus.

The old muscle car careened around the corner, jumping a curb and screeching to a halt just inches from the front door of the Rock's nightclub. The door swung open and out stepped an overweight bouncer with a black t-shirt stretched over his overweight belly, like a bear on his hind legs. Archie never bothered to learn his name, but knew his type. A bully, never challenged because of his size.

The bouncer pulled his shoulders back to shout as Archie came around the front of the car. "What in the flying fuck do you think you're doing? You had better get this fuckin' car out of here before I whoop your ass."

Archie didn't answer nor did he slow his stride toward the entrance. He just tossed his keys to the bouncer, who reflexively reached up to grab them. When his eyes were diverted, Archie grabbed the giant in both hands by the back of his thick neck, interlocking his own fingers and locking his elbows, creating a formidable hold. Then, in a swift and powerful movement, he jerked the bouncer's great head from its high perch, bashing the chin against the thick bone of his own forehead. Bryon called the chin the, "knockout button" effective as it was to put an opponent to sleep. Archie stooped now over the unconscious heap to retrieve his keys from the sidewalk, but before he could stand upright, a wave a nausea swept over him, starting in his forehead and settling deep in his gut before rebounding, rising through his abdomen. He vomited the yellow intestinal bile of one who had already exhausted the contents of his stomach and was now draining the innards. While he didn't feel remorse for striking the bouncer, who he saw do the same to fun loving customers on a daily basis, he felt some regret that the black t-shirt was now absorbing his puke, an unintended insult to injury.

Joe was at his cluttered desk using a paper weight to grind small pills to powder, pausing in annoyance when he heard the knob of his locked door gently turn in attempt to enter.

"I said I wanted to be left..." he started, but was silenced by a crash of metal on metal followed by the knob clattering to the floor a mere instant before Archie kicked the door open and entered, carrying the small bar stool he had used breach entry. Archie tossed the stool against the wall, shattering the framed pictures which hung there to cover the holes in the dry wall. He took several malice filled steps towards Joe who was quick to palm the pistol from the stack of pornographic magazines.

"Son of a bitch," Joe cursed, pointing the weapon at the Archie who had raised his hands but was still slowly moving forward, closing the distance.

"Careful, Joe. That's not the first gun to be pointed at me," Archie warned, speaking the truth. He was emboldened by the ever present deficit of respect in Joe's eyes and determined to disabuse it. Archie knew the highest form of respect was admiration, but the lowest form was fear and it was clear to him that Joe had neither.

The snide remark in the face of his handgun only

enraged Joe farther and he spat, "It might just be the fuckin' last, hotshot!" The pistol gave Joe over confidence, and in his anger he stepped closer to Archie to shove the gun in his face for emphasis. This was what Archie had intended. Moving all at once, Archie seized the pistol and pivoted, moving his head out of the line of fire while twisting Joe's knuckle in the trigger guard.

Joe screamed out in agony, feeling the bone in his finger flex to the point of breaking and forcing him to release the weapon. He collapsed somewhat meekly into his chair, surprised by the sudden shift of dominance and his loss of power. For dual purposes, Archie did not remove his eyes from Joe as he ejected the ammunition and disassembled the weapon, letting the pieces clatter to the floor. The first was a matter of his training and security, but the second was so he could savor the dawning realization on the club owner's face. For too long, a condescending Joe had regarded Archie as beneath him, unable to see that the young fighter was beyond him.

"Who do you think you are?" Joe yelled, embarrassed to hear the involuntary tremble in his own voice.

"It's not a matter of who I think I am...it's who *you* seem think I am, someone you trifle with."

"Look, I'm sorry about Byron. But Heckman is an animal! I have no control over him."

"We're all animals now, Joe."

Archie kicked Joe's chair in the spot between his legs, pushing the wheels to roll the subdued club owner into the corner of the office. Archie felt empowered to finally fight those who would have him battle for their cause and yet risk nothing themselves.

"You know what? To hell with you. Byron too. You're no better than me. A bunch of hypocrites"

"That's just it, Joe. We get in that cage and we

bleed for what we believe, but you just sit back and make your living off someone else's pain."

Archie removed a large photograph from the wall, a picture of Joe many years ago with boxing gloves hanging around his neck and a championship belt draped over his shoulder. He tossed the portrait onto Joe's lap. "The concept can't be entirely foreign to you."

Joe took the photo in his hands and stared at it, the familiar stranger looking back. The frame had protected the photograph well. It had not faded or torn, but rather it was the hands grasping it which had. Archie almost felt bad for his nemesis as his shoulders slumped and he suddenly appeared much older, almost feeble, as is prone to happen to one who has long since denied their age and only accepts it all in an instant.

"You might not believe it, but I was a lot more like you back then, kid."

Archie tapped the television screen which was

mounted in the corner above his head which displayed the progress of a horse race. "I gamble with my life and my heart, but you, Joe...you've been wagering your soul."

Joe tossed the photograph onto his desk and into the powdered drugs. Defeated, he took his head in his hands.

"The more money I made, the more I wanted. I made one bet too many. I barely own this place anymore! I owe to the same guys who bankroll Heckman."

"How much?"

"Too much. But as long as I let him fight here, I'm in good standing. They want to keep him tuned up, you know? Until his suspension is over and he can fight pro again. In the meantime, I make some money off the deal. It's not as evil as it sounds, Junior."

"Maybe we can help each other out, Joe."

"What are you thinking?"

***

Joe sat alone in a reflection so deep he didn't hear the squeal and rumble of the Pegasus leaving in the same furious manner it had arrived. He plucked the tray of powder drugs from the desk and disdainfully dropped it into the waste basket. The bouncer stumbled into the room, puzzled and covered still with Archie's dried regurgitation.

"What the hell happened to you?" Joe demanded. "Never mind. Call the boys in. We've got a fight tonight."

CHAPTER TWENTY-TWO

Meaghan was reciting the definitions of personality disorders for memorization while driving home, absent to the radio playing lightly in the background until a word snapped her out of her mental exercise. She turned the volume up, tensing as an on air personality blared, "Get your tickets at the door for the Downtown Beatdown. The undefeated Champ, Heckman the Ghost will finally take on the crowd favorite, Archie TNT!"

She whipped the car into an illegal U-turn with one hand while dialing her phone with the other. .

"Come on, come on." She heard the phone click and started talking before realizing she had only received the voicemail. "You've reached, Archie. I'm unavailable at the moment, but please leave your name, number and if applicable, your bra size and how you rate yourself in bed.

"Damn it, Archie!"

***

Archie was moving around the Argo, hastily packing a duffle with fight gear and equipment. Typically this was the time before a fight when he would dine on a small but hearty meal along with copious amounts of water. This time he neglected the victuals for none had passed his throat since he had laid eyes on his friend's battered body. It was only revenge which could bring him nourishment now.

As he stepped on to the deck, he stiffened, tensing as though his foot had landed on a mine that his next movement would detonate. The atmosphere carried familiar properties, immersing him in such virulent nostalgia that he was, for an instance, confused as to where and when he was. The hot air was heavy and thick. Nearby and down the shore, someone had thrown trash into a bonfire. All of this combined with his present state of mind was enough to bring him back to the battlefield. To his left was a naked toddler standing on a garbage heap in Afghanistan. To his right was a starving, limping puppy in Iraq. He could spare no pity for either. He could only move forward.

When she approached from the dock, Meaghan could read from his stoic body language that he was already at war. The knuckles on his dominant hand were split and his hair disheveled. Likely the last time he was in such a frame of mind, it was cropped short in military fashion and required none of the attention which was devoted solely to professional bloodshed.

They both paused at the sight of the other, steeling themselves for their collision as two surging rivers meeting for the first time, crashing together in calamity. Then Archie moved determinedly in his direction, avoiding her gaze deliberately. As a matter of principal, he was not given to explaining his decisions to others, no matter their displeasure at the course he charted for himself. He was his own master and slave to no one while others were captain of their own misery or happiness.

"Don't, Meaghan."

"Don't what?"

"Try and talk me out of it."

"So it's true then? You're really going to fight Heckman?"

Archie didn't answer as he opened a cargo hatch, looking for his mouth piece, but Meaghan understood his lack of an answer to be the one she dreaded.

"Why in God's name?"

He slammed the hatch down angrily. "Haven't I done enough in God's name? This...you should go to the hospital. See Byron. Heckman tore him apart. He's lucky to be alive."

"I'm sorry, I didn't know that. I know you love Byron, but you can't do this, Archie. Literally, you can't. You're not well."

Archie dismounted the Argo and took Meaghan's hand briefly, finally giving her eye contact. "This has to be made right and I'm no man of inaction. I have to do something."

"But you don't have to do this, Arch. Can't you just sit on the sidelines, just this once?"

Could he? He felt a man only had two options in life. He could decide his destiny and take it by forging it himself, or he could stand by and let fate choose one for him… a vacant fate no one else wanted to own. He considered that doom. All men were destined to die. There was no choice in the matter, but while his heart beat there remained some measure of volition. He looked pleadingly at Meaghan, desperate for her to understand this was him taking control of whatever was left to his life and choosing. "I don't want to sit here and wait for the cancer to make up its mind, Meg. I just...I-I can't be idle!"

"Archie, he's bigger than you!"

Archie recoiled, wounded. "He puts his faith in the needle and you want to call him the bigger man?"

"You know what I mean, Arch. If this was a legal fight with sanctions and weight classes you'd never be allowed in the cage with him. You can't win! I love you, but it's impossible!"

Archie bit the inside of his cheek to stop himself from speaking so he could form his words more carefully. She was right, to a point, for height in inches was the only standing most men would ever achieve yet he did not consider himself most men. When he was ready, he spoke. "You know I think you're something special, Babe. You hit with your words. Me, I hit with my hands and truthfully, I don't know which of us hits harder sometimes. But when it comes to the cage, you know nothing of the measure of a man. You see things in terms of size. I know better. I know my true stature. I know myself."

"That's just your ego talking now."

"Even the ego has something to say sometimes, Meg," he retorted, walking past her toward the parking lot, but he knew this was more than another bout. It was more than getting his hand raised high in the air. The stakes were too high this time, but he had too many wrongs left unchecked in his life and could not tolerate another.

Meaghan pursued him. "Archie, you just had chemo! The brain cancer, my God, he could hit you once and kill you!"

"I know, Meaghan."

"Archie, you'll die!"

"I'm not afraid of that."

"Maybe you aren't, but I am! I'm terrified to live without you!" This she directed more to God than Archie, a vain plea, for she knew that there was not a voodoo deity who would override Archie's actions, nor a pagan master who would intervene to stop him. Archie's will was inviolate, for better or worse.

He stopped walking to confront Meaghan, dropping his duffle at their close feet. It seemed his life was to be short and despite all of his fighting, he felt he had yet to vie for something he could be proud of. He had spent too long on the precipice of becoming something or nothing. Fighting campaigns that were not of his desire, but of others'. Finally, he would take up arms for his own causes. Not for God or country, but for Archie. Even if the cancer abated, this may well have been his last chance to give his name some measure of honor before it was carved into his headstone.

He would gladly sacrifice all to accomplish

some great altruistic feat. If there existed giant deities enthroned on Olympus, he would scale that mountain and tear the robes from their stone bodies, even if they crucified him, pinning him to a rock for all eternity for his deed of bringing light to humanity. But he was not a Titan. He was a man and while he could not make the world right, he could right the world around him.

"Look, don't confuse my lack of fear for death with contempt for life. I want to live! I'm still young and I'm not even done becoming me yet. But I'm more afraid of living a life I'm ashamed of than of living a short one. God, so much of my life has been spent in waiting, waiting for the chance to show what I'm made of. Here's a shot, and I can't let it pass me by! I've never been one to pull my punches don't ask me to start now."

"But what about me? Do you even love me? As a real person with real feelings, not some numb, pretty little object?"

"Meaghan, I don't even love my boat as an object! You, I love more than...well, so much it's probably a sin." He brushed her hair behind her ear, suddenly stumbling upon the answer to the problem she had presented from the beginning. He noticed when she was around it felt as though his brain was lazy and idle, as though it was not *thinking* as much as normal. It perplexed him until this moment when he realized this is what it meant to be content, to not always have his mind preoccupied with trying to solve some botheration or settle his doubts. It had been so long since he knew any measure of peace, he no longer recognized its presence. When she was around his world became smaller, quieter and more manageable. Yet while he may have been unaccustomed to such repose, he was well acquainted with the state of war he existed in now. This conflict was brought upon him when his most sacred territory was trespassed. His family, his brother, Byron. He loved

Meaghan, but to sit idly by now would mean loathing himself forever.

He believed a man was defined by how he ordered his loves. Two men could hold the same things dear: family, country, God, work, friends and themselves. But the man who put work first would be different from the man who put family first. That Archie could shove himself aside for his love of Meaghan, did not diminish it.

"Our time together has meant more to me than you can know, Babe…but now you're asking me not to be me! To turn my back on what I know is right. You already have my heart, Meg. You don't need my soul."

Meaghan tore Archie's hand from her face. "I can't let you do this. You're going to die!"

It didn't feel that way to him. Living a life always fearful of death and risk, playing it safe to avoid calamity…that wasn't living to him. It was the very slowest of deaths. He wanted to tell her, but knew it would fall on ears made deaf by love. He stooped for his duffel and marched away.

Meaghan called after him, "Archie!" But he didn't even slow his gait. Taking a deep, sobbing breath she wailed, "Achilles!"

Hearing her harrowed voice utter his primordial name, Archie froze, allowing Meaghan to catch up and stand in front of him.

"I'm not going to sign on to this - a life with a man that does whatever he wants regardless of how I feel. If you want me, you can't put me through this. So you choose right now. You choose me, and the life that comes with it. The whole thing! Or you walk away, and you keep fighting, shouldering some burden no one asked you to carry in the first place...If it's the latter, I won't be yours in the morning."

The vertebrae in his spine stiffened at the

challenge of an ultimatum, bracing itself for the collision hubris demanded it endure rather than ever submit. The greatest capitulation he could offer now was, "I'm sorry I hurt you."

Meaghan wiped her eyes dry. "I'm sorry I let you."

As she spoke, she loathed to love him. She felt broken, as though she had bent herself into the shape a key which might open Archie, but had snapped when turned. There was a portion of her within that lock she could not reclaim. She presented him with a future, but instead he embraced the past he had hitherto wrestled with and he was gone, devoured by the hungry soldier he carried within.

CHAPTER TWENTY-THREE

Archie was sitting on a keg in the Rock's dressing room, struggling to wrap his hands with white medical tape. A wave of weakness rose up from his bowels and spread to his limbs causing him to fumble and drop the roll. The chemotherapy was hitting him now with a force of exhaustion so heavy it felt as though he were aging years. He grabbed the hair on his temples which he imagined were sprouting elderly grey wool.

Intuitively, he recognized the distinct taste of the moment as a warning from the God which lurked above. A final reminder of what he stood to risk in this bout…his very life. He looked up, past the swaying, flickering light and communicated to this deity his defiant reply in a mental image: a leaping Greek man, shattering a plate beneath his dancing feet. This was his fragile body which he would now break himself rather than surrender it to the forces of order and chaos to protect or destroy at their whim. If this scorched earth policy was to be his final order, so be it. It mattered more to him that his life was his own to command, even to destroy, than in servitude to another who would drop the axe at their convenience, not his. He would prefer death to submitting his autonomy, his freedom.

"It's all set, kid," Joe said, breaking Archie away from his insolent communion.

"If you screw me on this, Joe..." Archie warned, leveling a stern look through the dark, tired rings around his eyes.

"Forget it, this is good for both of us," Joe assured him from the doorway. "Hey, you look like shit! Why are you so sweaty?"

Before Archie could answer, Mackey excitedly pushed passed Joe. "Geez Louis!"

"Calm down, Thelma," Archie grinned weakly at the old joke but it didn't seem to register with his baffled friend.

"Arch! Why didn't you tell me you were doing this?"

Joe laid a heavy hand on Mackey's shoulder. "Hey, get some water into him, he looks like a TKO waiting to happen. I gotta check on things."

Mackey examined Archie in disbelief. "I would've brought the corner gear if I knew you were fighting."

"I won't need a corner man, Mack."

"Don't be stupid. You'll need someone between rounds."

"This is going to be a one round fight, one way or another."

Mackey took a knee and scooped the roll of tape off the floor as Archie was struggling to reach it. Hastily but expertly, he began to tape one of Archie's hands.

"Thank you."

"Don't mention it, bro."

"Nah, I mean, for not trying to talk me out of this."

"Heckman...yeah, well, Meaghan called me. Left a pretty pissed off message...If those big tits can't talk you out this, I know I can't. Anyways, God trusted you with a will of your own for a reason. Besides that, my granny used to always tell me something. She said, the loveliest sound was that of a shut mouth."

Archie nodded, smirking slightly. "That's...that's beautiful, man."

Mackey paused his handiwork. "What? That's what she said."

"Nah, it's good really. It's like Twain or Thoreau."

Mackey went back to wrapping Archie's hands.

"You're an asshole."

"I know."

"Anyways, here's what I'm thinking. Heckman's defense is on point. You're going to have a tough time getting past it."

"I didn't imagine it'd be easy."

"Thing is, I've been watching him and he's a showoff. Kinda of like you. Only you do it before you win. He does it after. So *pretend* to be hurt. Let him think he's won and he'll lower his guard to make a show of it. And that's how you'll get in."

***

Archie climbed the few steps to the curtain area backstage, bemused to find the steps he usually bounced up now pumped lactic acid into his thighs. He was hoping the effects of the treatment would have diminished by now, but it seemed to be getting worse still. He mouth dropped to find Soko looming at the stair landing. Archie was about to speak but was preemptively silenced when Soko grabbed his face with a speed Archie could not have diverted. With his other hand Soko traced his thumb from the corner of Archie's forehead to diagonally between his eyebrows and down the other cheek, smearing black paint across his pupil's face while his crutches dangled from his forearms. When he was done, Archie was adorned with a single lightning bolt emblazoned in black across his face, a symbol to bring both speed and power to a warrior. Then, with a final stoic stare which imparted the words he did not speak, Soko hobbled down the steps and was gone.

Archie stiffened, sensing a new presence in the wake of his master which manifested across the stage as the white hoody of Heckman appeared in the dark.

They stood apart and formidable as two great mountains in unmovable opposition. Heckman's summit was ice and snow while Archie's volcanic peak had given way to the molten rage beneath. Their silent confrontation was interrupted by the announcer, "Ladies and gents, the hour has arrived!"

Heckman stepped into the center stage, closer now by half to Archie as the sound of chairs and sneakers squeaking signaled the crowd was rushing forward to the cage. Now within ear shot Heckman addressed Archie, "How's your friend?" He had cast the first spear in hopes of piercing his rivals' heart.

The snide comment manifested a mouthful of hate filled saliva which Archie spat on to the floor before he could parry, "You're about to find out."

"I thought he'd be better. I thought he'd fight like you."

"You'll know how I fight soon enough."

Heckman shook his head. "I'm not interested. That hospital visit got the police involved. I don't need the heat. I'll make you a deal...you play by the rules tonight, and so will I."

"You couldn't possibly play by the rules. The

cheating is already in your blood," Archie bit, alluding to the steroids. It was too late for Heckman's cowardly capitulations and his synthetic blood could make no recants. Moreover, Archie's own lust for vengeance could respect no promise of sportsmanship. As far as Archie was concerned this bout was the godless business of two man-animals. They were warring heathens, without rules, civility or even God. While he stood himself as detestable Sodom, Heckman was wretched Gomorrah and they would both be scorched from the earth for their effrontery, a price each was willing to pay if just to watch the other burn. Archie hoped there would be a new Genesis in the wake.

The announcer's metallic voice boomed, "This guy needs no introduction, but in case you live under a rock, I'll give it to you. At 5'10 inches tall, weighing 185 pounds, it's about to get awfully spooky in here... make some noise for Trey, the Ghostman Heckman!"

Heckman sneered at Archie and spread his arms out as though he were Atlas as the stage light beamed on him and an, "O Fortuna" remix shook the floor. As he stepped away he spat, "See you soon, you Greek freak."

Archie bore daggers into his foe until he stepped past the curtain and then slumped on the wall, bracing his palms against the tacky brick surface for support. The fight had not yet begun and the verbal toe to toe had fatigued his sick body.

He propped his shoulder blades against the wall and slid down, allowing the gritty surface to scour his back of dying skin cells, hastened to death as they were by the flow of the near toxic medicine coursing through his organism. He was slumped with his head by his knees, feeling more inclined to climb into bed than the cage which awaited him. His symptoms seemed beyond the side-effects of the chemo, alarmingly so, and for an instance he forgot his appointment with destiny and considered calling an ambulance. Was he ready to sacrifice his body?

Normally Byron would be here to pray with him. He made the sign of the cross and thought to make an invocation himself, but he felt God was sitting this one out. It was in that moment Archie felt his brain lurch inside his skull, reeling against the boney cavern with a pain that blinded and deafened him. He saw his cell phone in his hand with the half-fingered gloves. Barely had he recognized the apparition as the hallucination it was, before the screen lit up with a text message from Byron which read, "Do not be afraid of those who can kill the body, but cannot kill the soul."

His vision returned as the painful aberration subsided and the announcer entered his ears shouting, "Ladies, and gentlemen, but especially ladies...put it together for T-N-T!"

Archie filled his lungs with air and slapped his

face in an effort to restore his being to proper functioning like a frustrated mechanic berating a cranky engine. The spotlight beamed just beyond the curtain, waiting for him to possess it. He heard the first few beats of his song of choice and his spirit swelled with cockiness the tune instilled. He stepped into the beam, winking at The Ghostman Heckman as the Ghostbusters theme song announced him.

He was in character now, strapping on the feather light armor of an easy smile and bouncing step. He felt the confidence of one who had already forsaken all he could possibly lose. He was the master of his environment as he circled towards his prey which was trapped like a diver in a shark cage. Heckman wore the gear and played the part, but war was Archie's natural habitat.

He skipped up the ramp to the cage door which was held open by Mackey. The corner man took the fighter's mouthpiece from behind his ear, fumbling with trembling hands as he pressed it into Archie's mouth. Feeling bad for his shaking hands, he put steadiness into his voice and said, "I've got faith in you, Arch."

Archie tapped Mackey playfully on the chin with a glove, mumbling through the mouthpiece, "Me too."

He went straight to his corner as the door was latched behind him, the familiar clang sounding like a cavalry horn preparing a charge. His heart battered and bruised itself, knocking against his ribs, a cage within a cage.

He tilted his head back to look upon the packed balcony which curved around half of the octagon. They were perched there in anticipation of gory blood and deliberate injury, like spectators on a surgical observation deck. They would bear witness from their elevated palisade to the deadly duel below while they remained well beyond reach.

As the referee took to the center of the stage, Heckman thumped his gloves together and heckled Archie, "You ready to die?"

"I'm getting there actually," Archie retorted with an odd calm settling over him. He was seething inside as he looked upon Heckman, but was comforted by a notion that all was right in the world. He and Heckman were matter and anti-matter, composed of the same mass but opposite charges, destined to destroy each other in a minor cataclysm.

The referee rolled his eyes, uninterested in the melodrama as he asked Heckman, "Are you all set?"

Heckman nodded his reply as he pounded his gloves together.

He started to repeat the same question to Archie, but never got the chance. Archie was already rushing across the cage with an immediate flurry of swings as soon as he was in range of his prize. Many of his punches missed entirely, but Heckman couldn't parry them all, nor could he easily volley himself.

Archie connected with a hard uppercut to Heckman's chin who seemed more surprised by the blow than actually compromised.

Heckman leaned back at the waist as though doing the limbo while delivering a straight legged kick to Archie's midsection. It struck like a torpedo, striking Archie below the surface in the depths of his bowels as it knocked him back several feet. Yet from the outside looking in the blow didn't seem to register as Archie pulled himself back to Heckman like a magnet. Normally, the body's response to pain was to shut down, to cease the harmful activity. But with practice and will, one could override this somatic response as Archie did now, so well versed was he in agony. Whatever advantage Heckman had in fabricated, chemical strength, Archie met with unbridled rage. The hot, salty tears of earlier now rained upon his enemy as pelting, stinging rain in a maelstrom of strikes. Heckman responded with an icy, plummeting hail which landed upon Archie with crater-making might.

"That a way, Arch, that a way!" Mackey encouraged as he rattled the cage.

His fury was great but the taxation on his stamina was also fierce. His strikes slowed enough for Heckman to slip in and clinch Archie, whipping him off his feet and tossing him against the fencing. Before Archie could find square footing, Heckman was upon him with successive blows which bounced Archie off the cage with each one. Archie struggled now to hold his fists, weighted terribly by the fingered gloves, in front of him like a heavy, bronze shield. He tasted the burning iron contained in his blood as it surged from the broken capillaries in his nasal cavity and down his throat.

Feeling his captive going weak, Heckman eased off to hold his arms mockingly in the air as though victory was assured.

Blood swelled beneath the surface of Archie's right eye, pressing the flesh above against his lid, blinding him. He shifted his stance, more square than normal to find Heckman in his hemisphere of sight as he circled back to him.

Heckman recognized the handicap and posed as though to throw a punch. Falling for the false telegraph Archie moved in the opposite direction but Heckman swept Archie's ankle instead.

Archie never saw it coming. He hit the mat hard, his head catching the brunt of the fall. He tried to get up but was stopped by a paralyzing pain which dropped him back to the mat. He ran a searching hand over the back of his foot...his heel. It was bruised and turning darker by the second.

Archie limped towards the cage with his one good foot, using it to pull himself up. Clutching the fencing, he tried to put weight on his heel but it answered with agonizing pain.

Tunnel vision was competing now with the swelling eye to blind him completely. He could barely see his gloved hand upon fence fabric and beyond it the crowd jeering with raised drinks in the hands.

Every capillary in his brain seemed to pulse with his heart as time slowed down until the brief intervals between beats became long pauses, the roar of the crowd stretching into a distorted yawn. The fencing changed in his hand from clean, black plastic coated wire to naked, dirty and rusted steel wire. Beyond the fencing, the crowd changed as well, into a rioting crowd of Iraqi detainees in yellow uniforms and black beards. Moving calmly amongst them he saw blue eyes highlighted against sun-darkened skin. They belonged to an insurgent had he killed in Iraq. In the instance before he pulled the trigger, he had noted the uncommon eye color and imprinted them permanently upon his mind. Now they were staring into him again, as though calling to join them in the hell to which he had sent them.

They disappeared in a gust of swirling sand which stung Archie as he looked over his shoulder for Heckman finding a haunting form instead. Diane was there in the yellow cotton dress she wore for their first stateside date. Her arm came up slowly and Archie stumbled towards her, reaching out himself, but when her arm came to its azimuth, it was a halting palm. There was a pleading in her eyes and then the sand overtook her and she was what she had been before…gone.

The cage and the crowd returned as time resumed its normal pace. Heckman stood there in Diane's place. Archie felt an irrational hate manifest within, as if Heckman had really usurped her. He pressed the seam on the inside of his glove against his swelling eye and jerked it, slicing the thin skin open. As the hot blood dripped down his check, the pressure inside his head dropped and his vision returned.

The bell rang, signaling the end of the first round, but neither fighter acknowledged it. When the referee stepped between them to end the round Heckman shoved him aside. Heckman made a dash to grab Archie's waist, but fell just out of reach, slipping on the mat slicked by Archie's blood. Barely were his knees off the mat when Archie closed this distance with a small hop ending with a shin kick to Heckman's cheek.

Heckman's head whipped back, his mouthpiece dislodging. He rose nonetheless and spoke with the flashing of bloodstained teeth. "You're going out in a body bag, you fuck," Heckman challenged, though in reality he was taunting only to delay the fierce contact and recover his senses.

Archie spat his own mouthpiece out. "Make my day, you bloody piece of shit." He stepped forward to deliver a right hook, but his fists hit only empty air. Heckman had bobbed and weaved to avoid the hook and rose back with a hook to Archie's temple.

When the punch landed, Archie heard a sound like a gunshot, Arabic yelling and Diane scream his name in panic. He stumbled backwards, reeling from the blow and for an instant he saw Pastor Bob bellowing from the pulpit, "He who lives by the sword will die by the sword!"

Archie stumbled farther back now, grabbing his head while seemingly oblivious to Heckman who stood over him, confidently poising his fist in the air to deliver a lethal strike to the back of Archie's head.

Mackey breathed from outside the cage, "God, no, please." It was an instant replay of the night before and he could not stand by helplessly again. He moved towards the cage door, lifting the latch but was shoved aside by Heckman's corner man. Mackey returned the shove but adding a slug for good measure. He swung the door open, could only look on in horror. He was too late. Heckman swung.

Archie knew he was in peril and that raw, life threatening violence inspired intuition in him. He operated without thinking, but still knowing. Archie moved his head a fraction of an inch at the last second. When Heckman's punch sailed past him, he snatched it from the air and hugged it to his chest as he tossed his own weight towards the mat. Heckman lost his footing as Archie's weight pulled him down. Before he had completely landed, Archie was already twisting on top of him.

Archie trapped his rival's fist in his armpit and other arm between his own legs, snaring Heckman in the Crucifix. Heckman strained against the technique but to no avail. He was at Archie's mercy.

"Right, Arch! Tap him out, tap him out!" Mackey coached from the open cage door way. At the same time, a crowd member clung to the fencing near Archie screaming with bloodlust into his ear, "Break his fuckin' arm, TNT! Break it!"

Archie grunted and lifted his hips off the mat, putting pressure on Heckman's arm at the elbow. Heckman hollered in agony but nonetheless refused to tap in submission.

"Come on, snap his arm in two!" the crowd member demanded while Mackey still urged him to the contrary. "Archie! Just tap him out and let's go home!"

Archie glanced up at the crowd member, who seemed to beg Archie to admit his sins and own his brutality, as though the cage between them was the screen at a confessional

Archie made eye contact with Mackey and

shook his head. For an instant, Mackey was puzzled, but then he understood. "No, Arch, no! Turn the other cheek! This is when you turn the other cheek!"

Mackey was right. Archie knew what the deity above wanted, but he had demands of his own. Archie was not God, but nor was he a sheep. He was a man with sharp teeth and a windpipe that could shout, "No!" to the heavens above. Those who crossed him would be the subjects of his wrath. When he looked once more at his captive, he was astonished to find the visage fixed there was his own. He nearly lost his grip in surprise, but in regaining it he increased torque on the limb. As he looked into his own begging eyes, he understood full well the price of what he was about to do.

With a quick grunt, Archie lifted his hips off the mat, flexing his back until only his shoulder blades touched the ground. All the while he clung to Heckman's outstretched arm, causing it to move in the one direction while the elbow did not. The sickening pop of the joint giving way was accompanied by Heckman's pitiful wail. Only then did Archie release his defiled prey, when the body had been torn. Heckman would never fight again. The joint would heal but it would never be the same. Moreover, it was the physiological injury, the lasting trauma which would end Heckman's fighting career for good.

Archie was half dead and his foe was broken. Even the crowd had been reduced to an array of idiots behind cellphones trying to record the carnage, while the cage flooded with corner men and entourage. A heavily tattooed girl in medical gloves attended to Heckman while Mackey helped Archie to his feet.

Outside the cage a belligerent guy in a polo shirt pushed through the swarm to get a closer look, accidently spilling his drink on a ditsy girl who shrieked when the cold beverage doused what little clothes she had.

"You slob, look what you did?" she squealed.

The belligerent burped, "Like I care. You owe me a drink, bitch."

"Hey, asshole, that's my girlfriend!" an idiot behind his cell phone yelled.

"Then you two are one ugly fuckin' couple."

The idiot punched the belligerent, sparking a brawl which became club wide in a matter of seconds.

Mackey was struggling through the battling crowd towards the dressing room, while Archie clung tightly to him. Mackey looked back at the cage as beer bottles and chairs flew through the air and then ducked to avoid a soaring wig. "Hey, we may have actually been safer in the cage for once!"

"Mackey, get me out of here," Archie urged.

"Don't worry, nobody is going to mess with you after that fight, Arch."

"Mackey, I can't see."

"What?"

"I'm blind."

It happened before he even left the cage. He had blinked and when his lids reopened his sight was gone. Because of the chaos surrounding them, and his sudden impairment, neither of them noticed Meaghan struggling through the crowd to reach them.

She had spent the evening pacing back and forth in her apartment with a bottle of cheap wine and mascara falling down her cheeks. At some point in her drunken fog it occurred to her that Archie had never asked her to stop stripping. He never judged her for it, or even implied a problem. He understood that it was something she said she had to do and that was enough for him. He needed no other justification and never made any demands. The realization brought a heavy guilt. She had asked him, no, she had demanded he not do what he believed he must. She had accused him of being an egomaniac, yet it was she who tried to control him, delivering the ultimatum that kept her from being at his side when he really needed her.

It was this passionate insight which brought her to the club and through the thick crowds. She had shouldered her way past an obvious prostitute to reach Archie, and standing before him now, she had yet to think of what to say. When Archie's eyes fell on her, they were blank, devoid of any recognition of a partnership they had previously held. She was about to cry out, "I'm sorry" but to be looked at as a total stranger by one she felt so close to was more than she could bear. She choked on her own throat and turned away, wounded and ashamed. She disappeared into the crowd while Archie sniffed the air as Mackey tugged him along. He thought he smelled her perfume in the black, blind void but wrote it off as a symptom of missing her and nothing more. He wondered if he would ever see her

again.

CHAPTER TWENTY-FOUR

He lay on the mechanized table which whirred and clicked as it fed him into the MRI machine. Told implicitly not to move, he posed as though this was a dress rehearsal for his funeral and the padded tray beneath him his casket. In his blindness he could still sense the weight of the machine hugging the air around him, like a stone sarcophagus threatening to encapsulate him forever. He had never known claustrophobia before, and at any rate, the consternation he felt settling in could have been as much from his loss of sight as the artificial cocoon enveloping him. He knew panic was a hyper-fixation on fear, unchecked by the distraction rationale normally provided. Training had always taken over in combat, giving him minute tasks to focus on to see him through the firefight or match. To distract his dread he envisioned Meagan's breasts as the milky white orbs they were in the dark he was accustomed to seeing them in. The ideation calmed him like a distraught infant consoled by a familiar bosom. When a moment later a technician assisted him from the artificial tomb he thought he was still seeing those breasts, unaware at first that he was staring at the florescent lights above. His sight was returning.

Dr. Cavanaugh had ordered an emergency scan from his bedside when he received the call that Archie had been admitted. It was past three in the morning when he arrived at the hospital, by which time Archie was able to see well enough to make out that the doctor was still wearing his pajama pants and football sweatshirt under his white coat. Now that he seemed to be on the mend, he felt guilty to have inconvenienced the caregiver who was shining a pen light into his eyes.

"Everything is still really blurry. I can just see shapes, but I can tell it's coming back now. I'm sorry to have messed up your night, Doc."

"I don't mind getting called in, Archie. It's my job. But I don't like what you've done tonight." Cavanaugh seemed torn between two emotions as he spoke. His words begat disapproval, but his voice carried sincere sympathy.

"As long as my sight comes all the way back, no harm, no foul, right?"

"Just the opposite. You did real damage tonight. The tumor itself is bleeding. We've lost any real chance to operate, even as a last resort. It's just too risky now."

"What are you saying?"

Dr. Cavanaugh rubbed his hands anxiously and turned his back, consulting the images of Archie's head which were splayed on the steel table. There were three sets, a colorful one from his CAT scan, a black and white MRI and an equally abstract sonogram. Cavanaugh seemed to be deliberating with these as an attorney might approach the bench of a Judge to plead for a lighter sentence. Those three stacks seemed to stand unflinching as the Three Fates in their high mountain cave. Archie peeked over the doctor's shoulder at the table upon which his life had been spun, measured and cut.

When Dr. Cavanaugh addressed Archie again, he had the look of a beaten man. "Do you have a will? You need to get your affairs in order. And that means a power of attorney, someone you can trust to make some pretty important decisions once your mental faculties begin to fail."

"So that's what we're looking at then?"

"I wish I had some kind of good news. I just don't. If I led you to believe otherwise, it would be tantamount to medical malpractice. I'd be lying and I don't want to give you false hope.

Archie shook his head and chuckled sadly.

"It's okay, Doc. Every good fighter knows he

can't win them all."

CHAPTER TWENTY-FIVE

Archie sat in the hospital chapel, staring at the crossed pieces of wood before him which lacked the familiar form that was usually splayed upon them. They were painted white, he supposed so that all were invited to find their own meaning in what was claimed to be a non-denominational prayer room. Doing so, he pondered that perhaps these vacant beams were a seat saved for him, waiting for him to mount his final agony. The thought of being pinned by his limbs to such an afflictive fate was certainly on his mind. He wanted to rebel, but how could he? The cancer was coming for him like a billion miniscule crabs pinching him cell by cell, tearing him apart in a molecular frenzy. It was one thing to die, it was another to be destroyed.

Archie noticed the air in the room felt pregnant and wet as it usually does in the moments preceding a heavy rain. He was not then so surprised then when the stranger on the bench next to him broke the dark clouds that were overcasting his guise from the moment he sat down. Archie planned to let him cry in peace, feeling grateful the older man had broken the silence first and taken the burden up. Sorrow was a primitive language, monosyllabic and yet universal, such that it seemed to Archie he had no need to mourn himself with tears. All was being said that needed to be said. This man's sobs spoke for him and he did it better than Archie might have. There was something regal about how he cried, conservative enough not to be disdained and still free flowing enough to be admired. Archie studied him sideways until he placed where had seen the man's face before. It was on the billboard, for the luxury car dealership on the other side of town. As the venerable old man was not a model, Archie surmised he was the owner of the dealership.

"If you ever have any sons, they will cost you

quite a few tears," the man finally spoke, not apologizing but informing. Archie knew the man was speaking to him, not because he was the only audience, but because he felt acknowledged by him during his deluge as a fellow man.

The thought was painful for now that he knew with a certainty that he would never have any sons, he could imagine them with an acumen that rendered them all at once dear to him. The right side of his brain was reigning, allowing him to create them and feel parental love. They would be like him, only happier. Then they perished in his mind as a second thought careened between hemispheres, carried like a message on swift winged heels, bringing deductive logic and absolute truths. His children would never be, for Archie himself was soon to cease.

***

Archie left Byron's room, closing the heavy door carefully so as not to wake his mending friend. As he neared the hospital threshold, he could not help overhearing a dispute between the receptionist and the old man with whom he had spoken in the prayer room. The man was pleading with the receptionist over the exorbitant cost of his son's bill, an impossible sum levied upon him. Archie leaned on the receptionist's desk, trying to get her attention which earned him the annoyed response, "I'll be right with you, Sir."

Archie just shook his head and slid his credit card towards her, recalling the day he was less fortunate and a stranger proclaimed himself a friend. He put a hand on the old man's shoulder. "I want to pay his bill."

"Is that okay with you, Mr. Heckman?" she queried the man beneath his palm.

Archie withdrew his hand as though he had laid it upon a quilled back.

"Why would you…" Mr. Heckman started, taking notice of the stiches over Archie's swollen left eye. He had missed the laceration before when he sat to the right of his son's assailant. Then his eyes settled on the gym bag under Archie's arm, corroborating his suspicions.

"You hurt my son."

"He hurt my friend."

"And on and on it goes. Your friend is hurt. You're hurt. My son is hurt. And I'm hurt. It's a wonder the whole world isn't hurt. How can fighting ever end with that kind of thinking?"

"It ends when everyone is hurt," Archie replied bitterly, imagining that if all in that crowd had felt each blow shared between him and Heckman, all in attendance would have been less inclined to purchase a ticket. But as long as the fighting was done by the few while all the rest were able to spectate from a safe distance, there would be war.

"He's not a bad boy. I know he puts on a pretty good show. He may even get carried away sometimes, but he was trying to do a good thing tonight. He was hoping to win some money to keep the family dealership open a bit longer is all."

This revelation was the hardest hit Archie had suffered all night. Did he not also showboat, his cocky flirtation and bravado on par with Heckman's savage routine? He recalled Carl's broken shoulder, Heckman's snapped arm and even his own concussion suffered at the hands of his friend. Fighting was a brutal sport and even though he had good cause to fight for and had he not likewise, got carried away? He and Heckman were not enemies, but brothers.

As he beheld the father of his victim, all of his

rage, accumulated over a lifetime, turned to grief for having so well served his vocation. Soon it would be those who loved him who would stand in this father's mournful stead and there was nothing he could do to save them for he could not save himself.

CHAPTER TWENTY-SIX

Meaghan awoke cursing before she opened her eyes, recognizing the aftermath of a rough night as the precursors to a terrible day. That is, she was on the couch in yesterday's clothes and the temperature in the room meant the sun had been up for some time. She didn't want to open her eyes and face her hangover, but the movement of a strange animal by her feet jerked her to life.

"Olive! What are you doing here, girl?"

The dog gave no verbal answer, but seemed as dejected as Meaghan felt, as though they were both missing the same man.

"Archie?" Meaghan called hopefully, scanning the apartment. Her eyes came to rest on a foreign object on the counter. She rose from the couch to retrieve it, holding a handful of hair against her throbbing head. The amulet Archie had tried to give her once before now served as a paperweight for the letter beneath.

She deciphered Archie's poor penmanship with ease, knowing well the fingers of the hand which had grasped the lead and often traced her skin. The paper, marred with water stains around the edges from life as a live aboard, dropped from her hand as her face also fell. She snatched her keys and raced out the door.

***

Byron's lids broke the slight crust that had formed between his lashes overnight, a phenomenon that seemed correlative to the healing battered right eye which oozed thick tears. Looking to his bedside chair he felt a joy that could only be expressed by overt laughter. Draped over the back of the chair was the gaudy title belt of the Rock's nightclub.

The laughing made him aware of the envelope bouncing on his chest. Turning it over he read the simple and familiar axiom of his friend, "Eh." He understood at once that the pairing of the word and the belt meant Archie had shrugged off some burden. What he did not immediately comprehend was the envelope's content: a check made out to the church, a check which would save the church and a check signed by Joe.

***

Meaghan was expelled from her car by a force of paroxysm so fierce she nearly broke the door hinges during her hasty arrival at the marina. Her mind was racing nearly as fast as her feet as she darted under the overhang on her way towards the docks. She hadn't finished reading Archie's letter when she bolted from her apartment. Between her psych studies and love of the man, she intuited what the letter meant before it concluded. The words rang across her panicked mind now as though spoken from Archie's lips rather than inscribed by his hand.

I know this seems selfish to you. If I thought

wasting away in front you would help you, I'd have stayed and suffered. Try to remember that happiness passes and pain fades. Nothing will last forever and it is better to know this than wish it wasn't so. Everything comes to an end. Myself included, Meg. I will pass and I will fade away and that's okay. And I guess, I just don't want to die a Greek who never saw Greece.

She slowed her pace as she came down the dock and towards the Argo's slip. At the same time she remembered running off the school bus as a kid and slowing the same way when her childhood home looked absurd and different. The big elm tree in her front yard which she loved to climb every day after dinner was gone. It had been felled by her father who had noticed that it had begun to rot and die from the inside, but he had overlooked what the adored timber meant to her. She had no warning and was not prepared to see her playmate disappear without a farewell. The empty air which hung in the place the elm had once filled seemed

eternal to her child's mind, like the black void created

when a sun collapsed. Meaghan fell to her knees now

before the vacant space of water where the Argo usually

floated, and cried the heart wrenching cry of a little girl

whose favorite tree had been cut from the earth.

CHAPTER TWENTY-SEVEN

Archie scrambled over the deck to lower the mainsail by tugging the halyard line down, hand over hand. The sail flapped near his face as it dropped, luffing in the light breeze that blew off the beaches of the Bahamian island. A better and sober sailor could have made the trip in three days, but it had taken Archie twice that.

Deprived of its mainsail, the Argo slowed as its inebriated captain stumbled off the foredeck and retook the helm to put her back on course. He took up the binoculars he stole from the military and scanned the coast for the customs port, using them as a monocular by spotting through one eye in an attempt to narrow his drunken vision. A frown formed when he spied a beach full of lounging tourists in white and red skin as the techno music of the beach bars reached him from across the water. Humans in their unending quest to be comfortable had become decadent and severed from the harsh realities of nature. He felt disgust at the sight and considered forgoing this stop for provisions.

He had enough fresh water if he didn't waste any for bathing, and he could stretch the booze onboard by mixing it with his prescribed painkillers. Despite the natural inclination, he tried hard not to be a misanthrope in his life, for he knew every being originated from the same single seed, and therefore belonged to him as brother and sister. Yet he could not help but feel scorn for them at times when they seemed to fall so short of their common parent, bringing dishonor to a proud legacy. Now the effort seemed pointless and he was given to indulging this sentiment in the same way he was also drinking without compunction.

When a potato chip bag floated against the hull he cursed his entire species. Of course, the fat fuck who dropped the trash had no compunction, for having polluted his body, violating the shared Earth was of little concern. He was supposed to love his neighbors, but did they not forfeit the term when they ceased caring about the welfare of the community?

A fluttering near the helm announced the presence of a seagull. The company annoyed him at first for he wanted to be left alone, but the bird asked no questions so he tolerated its presence.

He dropped anchor as the sun was sinking below the waterline in a similar way. The strain of day seemed to exhaust him disproportionately to what he felt it should which he took to mean the cancer was working overtime, sapping his resources. He slinked below deck and turned on the light with a red bulb. He had no need to see in the dark, but found the regular bulbs harsher on his senses and more agitating to his migraines.

He curled on the floor beneath the soft beam, clutching his skull which was reeling with pain. He was drinking to keep himself from turning around and abandoning his crazy plan, hoping by the time he ran out of booze he'd be past the point of no return. The pressured pain within his skull was another reason. It felt like a wise little brat was trying to burst from his head. His brain seemed to dangle at the end of his spine like a marshmallow on a stick, roasting on the fire that was his nervous system exposed.

When he finally passed out, it was not from booze or the exhaustion, but from the utter agony.

***

At some point in his slumber he became aware that the Argo was in motion. Thinking the anchor had dislodged, he tried to rise to secure his boat but found himself pinned to the cabin floor by enfeebled limbs. With his head pressed against the boards, he listened to the wind and water move around his vessel and came to the conclusion, however impossible, that his sails were raised. In fact he could feel that they were in perfect alignment with the wind, and that these angles complimented the rudder below such that the boat sailed straight and fast without a pilot. Sailors called this phenomenon, "the slot" referring to the perfect conditions for which the engineers had designed the boat. Archie looked up from the cabin through the open gangway and watched the wheel make slight movements from left to right, keeping itself on a course of its own design.

He crawled to the hatchway stair and climbed unsteadily step by step until his nose hovered over the half empty glass of spiced rum he had left at the top. The drink revived his senses somewhat like an ammonia smelling salt, but he was still quite intoxicated. In this drunken delirium, he thought he saw a man at the helm, tall and deathly gaunt. He possessed the dead, white eyes of a recent corpse or perhaps a blinded man, but the deliberate and quick way the orbs moved in their sockets begat sharp sight. Archie boosted himself farther up the gangway until his head was level of the bare and gnarly feet which seemed rooted to the deck behind the wheel.

He was marveling that the mouth of this sailor was non-existent, only thin, white skin stretched over the space where one should have been, when the dead eyes fixed on him and spoke so that there was no need for lips to part. Understanding the silent demand perfectly, Archie raised his glass to this commandeer who bent his lengthy frame with a creaking like a great tree being pulled by its top to meet the ground. Close now, he wrapped his branch like fingers around the proffered libation and pressed it to the place where a mouth should have been, pouring the rum into the parched skin which flaked like birch bark. Satisfied that the fare was paid, the boatman resumed his task of delivering his mortal cargo in the hold below across this mighty river Styx.

Archie fell back to his previous place upon the floor, relinquishing command of his vessel to the Trade Winds which were pulling him towards the Dark Continent, a strong and sturdy Charon trafficking damned souls for damnable coin.

***

He awoke with a start the next day reaching for his rifle which used to lay as his bedtime companion on deployments. Neither he nor his weapon were present there, but he rose stealthily nonetheless palming the bowie knife he kept handy for intruders. He exited the cabin stealthily, on guard for the strange presence he had witnessed the night before. Only the gull was still there, a surprise in itself that it had remained for so long. The sails were as he had left them before his nocturnal convalescence and even the anchor line still appeared lowered. Had he imagined the visitor? No, he realized. It was much worse than that. He had hallucinated the encounter, a side effect of the swelling tumor. A drunken dream would have been more reassuring than knowing that his faculties were failing him at such a rate.

Still, he appeared far from where he had dropped the hook last night. Certainly the Argo had drifted a great distance without his steerage for he was now at the far eastern end of Grand Bahama Island, a distance of considerable travel. Craning over the bow he pulled on the anchor chain which answered with unusual levity. Coming to the end he found that he had lost the ballast altogether as the cotter pin which had always fastened it must have slipped loose. Not a common occurrence at all, though it explained his drift.

Normally the loss of the anchor would have constituted a concern for a mortal sailor, but Archie already felt severed from the tether of life. He lived now only to accomplish this self-assigned mission, a voyage which gave him something to fight when he could no longer challenge his antagonist directly. He smiled, remembering his friend who taught him this cathartic art of survival.

As Archie raised the sails his avian stowaway stretched its wings, holding them static so that the wind would pass beneath and tickle its downy pits. Then it cocked its head as though to question Archie's intent, but surmising the answer it pumped its feathered fins and flew off towards the island which the Argo was leaving behind. It had sensed that the point of no return was near and was abandoning the vessel which was on a collision course with destiny no being with a survival instinct would desire.

Archie pulled the lines taut, stretching the sails to their limit, like a fierce charioteer whipping frothing horses to their last ounce of speed and strength. Behind him he dragged a corpse, his own life spent which he was delivering himself to the Gates of Hell. The boat seemed to shrink around him as the ocean grew vaster. He could sense the hundreds of feet below him fall off into thousands of fathoms of dark abyss.

He recalled now the time he nearly drowned in his Popou's pool as a toddler. The orange floaties on his little biceps bloated his confidence, which moved him into the dreaded deep end of the pool where his toes could no longer touch. He felt brave there until the deadly hiss of the deflating devices announced his demise. No longer buoyant, but in fact heavy, the floaties dragged him down to the bottom of the pool. He screamed for help beneath the water, not knowing any better, only managing a gurgling which drowned him farther, a pathetic bubbling SOS no one could hear. He knew this was death, but then he felt a sharp pull on his scalp as his Popou pulled him to the surface. Here he was once more, swimming so far from sure ground, once again on the confidence of a device which may fail. Only this time, his Popou could not possibly be there to save

him.

CHAPTER TWENTY- EIGHT

A passenger plane outbound from Nairobi soared above the clouds en route to Madrid. The glowing yellow 30,000 feet below its underbelly had turned to a refreshing blue as it left the sun baked sands behind, crossing the strait. The plane, no longer subject to the thermal energy created by the scorching Sahara, resumed a comforting disposition. To the few who remained awake and crammed by the window, the view below was a blue chasm separating two jutting land masses. The white dot which bobbed in the blue below was barely discernible from this height.

***

A weather-beaten and bearded Archie sat at the helm of his ship which bobbed in the water without making headway. He was shirtless and his healthy physique was gone. A decade of medical school, a devotion to oncology and blood tests were all redundant for one to make out his illness. The cancer had progressed to a point that its presence was manifest.

He was completely lost in thought as he watched, through sunken eyes, a loose halyard line flap in the wind and smack repeatedly against the metal mast. He imagined seizing the line in his teeth and climbing a few rungs up the spar. He could balance precariously there as he fashioned a noose before slipping it over his head like a neck tie. Then he would step away from the mast, his body would fall and jerk at the end of the rope, snapping his sunburnt neck.

Ending the morbid fantasy, he rose wearily from the deck and seized the halyard line, looking at it with puzzlement, as though it was a gun that fired without his permission. He clenched it in a hand roughed by the days of working with rope, the tough skin creaking like the tight leather of a new mitt. He was trying to squeeze the life out of the line, as it had so tempted him, before he secured it to the bottom rung and returned to the helm. That death was not more or less ignoble than the one he had left behind, albeit it quicker. But to end it now seemed to disgrace all for which he had previously suffered, endured and been spared. Byron had called him a warrior once, as such he did not want to surrender any more than he wanted to wither away. He wanted to die fighting. Still he had to admit suicide had, like all moral debasement, a certain allure to the broken.

He lost sense of time during the many days of the bleak crossing and could not reckon for how long he had been a man without an anchor. His wristwatch he tossed overboard, no longer wishing to be lashed to minutes and hours. Having forsaken temporal existence he regained the animal rhythm which throbbed to the rise and fall of the sun. All the same, living imposed its own measurements for he was aware his body had become less musculature and more skeleton, as though it was already decomposing. Once when walking in the woods, he happened upon a snake who was regurgitating an earlier meal. The digested prey, a rodent of some kind, was reduced to a mass of bone and air, stripped of useful flesh. This was the image that presented itself in the mirror above the head that morning and it was the reason he smashed it, wishing instead to vanquish his own wraith which stared him back.

As a natural consequence of his objection to time, he had only an approximate notion of his location, having been sure only of his bearing and never taken measure of the distance traveled. So it was somewhat surprising to see the dark, hazy land masses appear on the horizon, one on each side of the bow. He held his hands before him, palms out as though bracing against those dark shapes in the distance and framing them in his vision.

"The Pillars of Hercules," Archie whispered,

referring to the Strait of Gibraltar, and addressing himself, a habit borne out of these days of soliloquy and solitude. He found consulting himself in this manner therapeutic and a wonder that of all the people to speak with in the world, he long neglected the one most dear to him.

To his port he would find a Spanish harborage, to the starboard, a Moroccan. Either would suit him, but neither broke his indifference on the subject. As the day was coming to an end, Archie left the decision to the ebbing waters which carried him towards the Strait. He would visit whichever port was nearest when the day began again.

Below deck, he used the last of his potable water to brew a cup of powdered coffee in the tin canteen cup he was issued in boot camp. When he returned topside, the night was already dark and full. The breaching of a whale sounded off his stern, like a trumpet full of spittle.

That the baleen was aware of the Argo before it announced itself, Archie had no doubt. But he pondered if the whale recognized the Argo was not a being, but in fact a vessel carrying a being. As the whale drew curiously closer, Archie surmised it was asking the same question. Was Archie a man aware that the whale was more than the fleshy fuselage which weaved through the water, and that there was indeed a being contained therein? Archie sighed and the whale answered with another spouting. They were well aware of each other.

CHAPTER TWENTY-NINE

The Argo was the only sailboat among a hundred small fishing boats in the large, floating dock complex of the Port of Tangier. The other side of the Port was teeming with mammoth sized cargo ships and Super Tankers. Archie was pacing the dock near the Argo, amused by his legs which seemed surprised to find steady ground after walking at sea for so long. Two Moroccan port officials emerged from the Argo's cabin, a look of displeasure apparent on their mustachioed faces. Archie was dimly aware that his hold stunk of body order and poor housekeeping. Annoyed and without pleasantries, they handed the foreigner back his documents and went to wash their hands.

A dark skinned boy of a dozen years watched them depart before waving to Archie from across the dock. "Pssst. You!" He called from his seat on the bench of a sea rotten fishing boat.

Archie answered with an annoyed glance, but the boy continued unperturbed.

"You America?"

"*Naam,*" Archie answered in the affirmative in Arabic.

"You understand Arabic?" the boy challenged in his native tongue.

"A little. Iraqi." Archie pulled his dog tags just above his shirt collar so the boy could see.

"Ah, you soldier! Where are going?"

Archie pointed to the east, "Greece."

"Because why?"

Archie thought for a moment and shrugged. He didn't have the words in Arabic to tell the boy he was chasing a destiny and running from a fate.

Not truly interested, the boy didn't push him farther, but stealing a furtive glace in the direction the port authorities left in, he lifted a blanket by his feet, revealing rows of Marlboro cigarettes.

"You cowboy. Want to buy?"

Not wanting entanglements with the Port Authorities over untaxed tobacco, Archie shook his head, the slight movement causing him to wince and rub his eyes.

The clever little smuggler countered, "Ah, head hurt." The boy moved the cigarettes aside and opened a metal tin full of marijuana in zip lock bags. "Hashish. Very good for head hurt. You buy, yes?"

Archie laughed at the proposition, but then considered. His own pharmaceuticals were depleted and his last half bottle of rum he was saving for what, he didn't yet know. He had never smoked the weed. It had never really occurred to him before either. An early career in the military forbade it from habit and thought. Now there was nothing barring him, moreover, the pain of cancer gave him a substantial reason to indulge.

Still, he told the boy no. His faculties were already compromised. Sailing was serious business and he needed to be of sound mind to accomplish his goal. For that, he would have to bear some pain. And that, he felt sure, for only a short while more.

He was beginning to appreciate what it meant to lose one's sanity as he felt increasingly absent his own. Before the cancer, his mind had been a garden, a refuge to which he could retreat in communion. His doubts, woes and fears were seeds he planted there, budding thoughts which bloomed precious revelations. Now they wilted in infidelity, for in recent days he had found himself thinking things he would never have allowed before, bad things, previously so against his nature, it was difficult to believe the ideas ever originated within his mind. It was more like someone else suggested them.

That very morning, while struggling to heave aboard the sea anchor, which was essentially a giant rubber bag filled with ocean water, he had begun to imagine an alternative activity. He saw himself coiling the anchor rope around his ankles and dropping the bag overboard so it could sink to the deep and take him along with it. Instead, he collapsed on the deck, panting from exhaustion and weeping from the vision. He could no longer tell if his mind was failing his body, or his body failing his mind. His body faltering in a mechanical sense, he could forgive, but the betrayal of his mind was the most personal treason.

He could no longer depend upon his psyche, for in one moment it would kiss him on the cheek, and in the next deliver him to execution. That his body and brain shared the same bread seemed of little difference to this corrupted organ.

CHAPTER THIRTY

The Argo crashed through the waves, making good speed as the wind tugged the sails along. Archie was on the top step of the gangway with his shoulders just above the hatch so he could peer down the compass held close to his eye. The heaving of his vessel made it near impossible for him to sight the island he was using as a landmark. He ducked below, taking his measurements to the chart where he traced a few lines across a ruler's edge.

He studied the chart, using parallel rulers and metal dividers to discern his location as he scratched his head in frustration. Given his course and speed, he should have been able to discover his location, but the lines and amorphous shapes might have been coffee grains in the bottom of cup, telling him a future he could not yet comprehend.

Giving up, he chucked the pencil across the

cabin and returned topside.

Twisting an arm around one of the lifelines that ran the length of the boat, Archie hung off the side so that he could scoop up a handful of water. Hoisting himself back aboard, he touched his wet hand to his lips, tasting. It kissed him back, laden with extra brine. It meant he had left the ocean far enough behind that he was now sailing on a sea, a sea he had longed for. The salt he tasted had been snatched by rain water from Greek cliffs, tossed down Greek valleys, pushed by Greek rivers and thrust into the Greek sea he know cleaved.

"I'm in the Mediterranean. I might actually make it."

***

Archie worked skillfully by the bright lunar light to slice the flesh from a fish he had caught. He was on his knees, filleting his catch upon an overly used cutting board. The species was unknown to him, a matter of little concern. It was sustenance, though as he carved the meat, he wondered if he was right to end this fish's life. Normally, he'd have thought nothing of it. After all, he was a man with a sentience so much longer and more meaningful than the aquatic animal that the act seemed just to sustain it. Then a budding thought spout that his life was now the lesser remainder. Left to a natural death, this fish would probably have outlived him and may even have procreated. And as for meaning, well it had no more meaning to him than the fish had to his own, for everyone he cared about in the world already took him for dead.

The moon glinted off the sharp blade, distracting him from his task. He paused his hands and brought the blade towards his wrist, aware that his flesh would sever as easily as the fish's had. He might have committed the heinous act, if his ears had not discerned a voice, hushed and barely audible, a whisper in the otherwise silent night which was void of the usual wind and waves. He abandoned the fish, searching for the voice, and in doing so, became aware of how eerily calm and flat the water was. The Argo made no motion, as though it was fixed on the surface which appeared hard as the moon reflected off it like the wax on a marble floor. He sensed with a certitude that he was being watched.

"I'm not alone."

When his voice broke the night, it startled a black bird from its perch on the masthead which retaliated with an alarming squawk. For a pause, Archie was assured the avian presence was the one he had sensed, but then his gaze fell to the bow and the figure which lurked there.

"Who are you?" Archie questioned, terrified to move.

"You know who I am," the Devil answered.

CHAPTER THIRTY-ONE

A badly battered Archie watched the sun rising through eyes deprived of the last night's sleep. The Argo was in complete disarray. Loose lines dangled everywhere and there was water up to his waist in the cabin. Supplies and belongings floated nearby, all carried in a stream as the sea carried them away in the same direction. He pulled the cork from a near empty bottle of rum, his left arm useless in a sling fashioned from the tattered blue canvas of what remained of his Bimini top. He finished the bottle in two swings. The first mouthful burned in his belly while he spit the second immediately into the gash etched across his right palm.

The events of last night should have left him shaken, but he never felt surer of himself for in today's dawn he was free of the thoughts of deliberate death which had plagued him of late. Before they had come to him like suggestive whispers, their speaker always concealed by the noise of the wind, sea, and his own thoughts. But last night, it was too quiet. The whispers gave the speaker away. He showed himself.

***

"You're Satan." Archie addressed the man who had appeared on his vessel the night before.

The man, leaning easy in the bow pulpit, rolled his eyes.

"Not my favorite appellation. I really much prefer my given name…Lucifer." His breath could be seen as he spoke, frosting the warm Mediterranean air. His pale skin nearly glowed in the night, contrasted even more by the charcoal colored, moth eaten fisherman's sweater. Albino white hair crept from underneath the wool of a fisherman's cap, more suited to a winter climate. Despite his borderline freakish appearance, he was beautiful, almost artificially so.

"This isn't real. This is the cancer. It's a hallucination," Archie told himself, refusing to address the man again for fear of solidifying him into reality.

Lucifer scoffed, "Achilles! Look around! Whether I am in your head or on your deck, it is still just you and me out here...or in there as the case may be. Reality is rather relative out here, isn't it?"

Lucifer pulled a moldy cigarette from a rusty case which squeaked as he opened it. The end of the cigarette flared up, lighting on its own when it touched the frozen blue lips. He shivered and inhaled luxuriously before continuing, taking his time as though relishing the confrontation as much as the tobacco.

"Is it of any more comfort to think your brain is in such an ill state as to concoct apparitions? What's more, of all apparitions, you would summon me?"

Archie covertly scanned for the knife he had been filleting a fish with a moment before, but it had disappeared from sight. Lucifer smiled knowingly as he placed a foot overboard and the sea rose to meet it. He walked on the water, closing the distance from bow to stern.

"See, I can do it too!" he said laughing, but the laughter seemed forced, like the choked bubbling of a stream trying to fight its way through a heavy layer of ice. His feet splashed lightly on the surface, as though he was stepping through a puddle until he paused abreast the Argo. The water beneath his feet froze solid, cracking and crisping with frost as he held his arms wide, just higher than his shoulders in a mock crucifixion, gesturing with open arms towards Archie.

"Do you accept me now, my son?"

"What do you want?"

"I want to save you, Achilles."

"I'm good, thanks."

Bemused, Lucifer relaxed his blasphemous pose

to flick his cigarette into the sea.

"I hate it when people say that."

Bending down to reach into the water, he scooped a translucent jelly fish into his hands which quivered as he cuddled it with hands that tightened around it as he spoke.

"You're not, "good" and you're certainly not healthy. That tumor of yours is growing, pushing your brain against your skull, squeezing it..."

Archie flinched as the jellyfish burst in Lucifer's hands, its dismembered and disemboweled bits squishing between the perfect white fingers. With a look of great concern, Lucifer held his hands up, the remains of jelly fish dribbling into the sea.

"I don't want to see you suffer, Achilles."

"Then don't watch."

"Don't do that. Don't have such a prejudice against me. I want to help you, and unlike God, I've left you alone until now. I've respected your will as your own, and I have not become wrathful when you strayed from me. I-I love you, Achilles. I really do. You are one of my favorite humans. You remind me so much of myself."

"I'm nothing like you. You just want to hurt people. That's not me."

"Oh, you haven't hurt anyone? I admit the work I do is not attractive, but it is necessary... I think you know something of this. And yes, I have brought harm to many. But I have also been on earth since the beginning of man, well, mankind as you know it at any rate. And I would argue that you have harmed an amount equal to my own in proportion to your mere mortal years here."

"That was different. That was war."

"And so is this a war. And the wars you fought were for what? Freedom? What is anarchy, but absolute freedom?"

"You're wasting your time."

Lucifer shook his head.

"Time is a human commodity I am unfettered with. You don't know it, but you called me here. Oh, I see the doubt upon your face, but it's true. When a person is as weak, as tired and near death as you, there's a stench like ripe fruit that beckons me." With this he stirred the air beneath his nose, inhaling it contemplatively as though preparing his palate for a fine wine.

"I don't fear death."

"Nor should you! It is living that causes you pain now. I came here to bring you this assurance...You can end your life, Achilles. There is no shame in it."

"There's no honor in it either."

Lucifer threw his hands up in exasperation.

"What is it about you that have to fight everything? Now even living has become a stubborn form of protest for you! This little rebellion of yours is unnecessary. You are suffering needlessly. And where is God? At least I made the trip."

"I'll meet my maker at a time of His choosing and not a moment before."

Lucifer batted the air in front of his face, dismissing the comment as one might an annoying insect. Archie backed to the portside of the boat as the devil stepped over the lifelines on the opposite side, kicking water off his shoes with disdain. Stepping into the cockpit, he hung one arm on the boom, leaning close to Archie who had moved as far he could.

Lucifer looked over his prey, appraising him, while the proximity caused Archie to shiver as he might in a winter wind. The fallen angel's presence was abstract, devoid of standing, like a void. It brought not company, but utter desolation. Archie had never felt as lonely as he did now in the presence of Satan.

Lucifer noted Archie's tremble and took a conciliatory tone. "Look at you, Achilles. He has left you in the cold, like me. Oh yes, He is light, He is warmth, but at what price? He offers shelter but only with submission. His light is tyranny, don't you see that? It takes courage to venture without the comfort He provides for limited freedom. I know. Now you are tired. Death can be your rest. You are in such pain. Please, take the relief that death can give you. There is nothing gained by living and nothing lost by dying."

"What would you know? You've never died before."

"I've known many who have."

"In hell?"

"Obviously."

"Then you've only known those who have fallen, not those who have risen."

Lucifer winced in annoyance, pulling his lips

back like a hissing cat. At the same time he ground teeth covered with a thin layer of frozen saliva which fell from his mouth like snow as he spoke, "Do not...do not preach to me. I know more about rising and more about falling than your literal human brain could ever comprehend. I am trying to help you. You, a doomed man with only two paths before him. And they both lead to death! Why choose the one of greater suffering?"

It was a fair question, one for which Archie had no articulated response ready. He had grown up poor, fought in wars and a few dozen cage fights. He had moments he was afraid to die and others when his heart was so broken he wanted nothing more. Suffering was nothing new to him and enduring it was a matter of habit. Archie halted this rumination, coming suddenly aware that the devil was having his way with him. He had received contingency training before his last deployment, preparing him for the possibility of becoming a prisoner of war. He recognized the tactic Lucifer employed, asking questions to deliver him to a presupposed conclusion, not his own.

Determined to refute his status as a captive and having a penchant for words tailored to the most personal and concise insult Archie spoke thus, "If Jesus could die for me, the least I could do is live for Him."

Lucifer recoiled as though the mention of Christ's name burned him, but in nearly the same second, he bared his teeth and lunged at Archie, seizing his neck and forcing his head over the Argo's side. His arms tied up in the lifelines like a boxer on the ropes, Archie fought against the clutch but the effort only caused his blood to seep from beneath Lucifer's sharp fingernails which dug in further. With the pupils of their eyes separated only by a few centimeters, Archie was able to glimpse into the fallen angel's marrow to see that as the ultimate egomaniac, Lucifer fancied himself the supreme deity. God's very existence was then a constant contradiction to his delusion, an inherent disproof.

Lucifer's rage redoubled when he realized his momentary transparency. Archie's self-awareness had forced him from the shadows where he was presently exposed. This mortal man had become like the eye painted on his hull, able to counter evil by seeing it directly. It was those who refused to acknowledge evil, preferring to pretend it did not exist in an effort to see the world as they thought it ought to be rather than seeing it as it was…they became his hapless victims. He could not so well deceive or manipulate those who realized his presence.

Ripping Archie's shirt open from the collar, he listened there as he slapped his ghastly palm against the exposed chest in time with the frantic heartbeat.

"That is not the heartbeat of a man so ready to die! Or does your flesh continue to betray you? Perhaps it is less willing to part with you than you are to shed it. I have always found the flesh to be a more reasonable compromiser than the soul."

His windpipe closed, Archie could make no retort, as a vessel in his right eye burst with a flash of red from the choked circulation.

Relaxing his grip, Lucifer said, "Well, that won't do."

Archie made a noise like a broken trumpet as he inhaled a full breath into empty lungs. Lucifer smiled, dragging a sharp nail across Archie's chest in the shape of a pentagram. Archie could not help but cry out in agony as his flesh was carved open.

"Ah, you see. I've been wasting my time on a stubborn spirit when the body is far more responsive."

Archie tried to speak, but he was on the verge of hyperventilating and his voice was reduced to a raspy whisper. Lucifer ceased his assault to give Archie some reprieve as he brought his ear closer to his victim's mouth.

After a few deep breaths, Archie managed, "Fuck…you."

Lucifer hissed, backhanding Archie and clutching his face so that he had had to look him in the eye as he shouted, "What you forget is that I knew your messiah! I was there when He suffered. I drove in the nails! And for all your heart, you are not the soul He was, Achilles."

With this, Lucifer took Archie's legs and flipped him overboard. Archie was quick to grab the rail of the boat with one hand, but struggled to get a hold with the other as Lucifer crouched above him.

"There. I've made it easy for you. Now all you have to do is let go. Your death no longer requires you to take action. Rather, it can be done by doing nothing at all."

As Archie struggled to heave himself aboard, Lucifer used his teeth to clean the blood from beneath his fingernails.

"In truth, I have acquired more souls from passive acts than misdeeds."

Feeling the panic that precedes drowning, Archie managed one last plea for divine intervention, "God…"

Lucifer cupped his ear, as though trying to hear a response. When none came, he shrugged in mock apology.

"Pathetic. I have seen every generation of man and yours is the worse to ever scour the Earth! For you are the first with the collective ability to save each other from the darkness of poverty and ignorance but are unable to do so only because of your individual selfishness! For you, the end of so much suffering is nothing more a dollar amount you leave unpaid!"

Lucifer raised his head back, screaming at the black sky with angry tears falling from his eyes.

"Do you believe me now? Have you not seen enough of this vileness you started with men?"

Lucifer continued his insane monologue, but Archie could not hear the words as his ears submerged. He was considering swimming to the transom of the boat where he might manage to bring the swim ladder down, but he knew he had not the strength left to swim even those few feet. His few fingers clutching the rail were the only thing keeping his head above the water, barely. He was afraid to move at all, for fear the next motion would be his end.

Through eyes, obscured by saltwater, he thought he saw another bird take perch on the spreader bars halfway up the mast. This time it was a white bird, a dove Archie thought, and the thought gave him a curious resolve, as though such a beautiful animal could not possibly bear witness to such a grim death, and therefore, it must be that he could not die in its presence. Trying his legs, his foot found a solid object. The top edge of the rudder, turned hard to port by the current, and come just with reach of when set of toes.

As he braced himself on this awkward footing, Lucifer renewed his interest in him. With savage bloodlust, Lucifer leaned over to push Archie's head beneath the water, an act he did not resist as his assailant came farther and farther overboard to do it. Then he used the rudder's edge as a step to shoot himself out of the surface of the water, past Lucifer's hips which he shoved behind him on his way onto the Argo's deck.

Archie crawled across the deck, climbing the helm to pull himself to his knees, searching for the devil he had thrust into the sea but he was nowhere in mortal sight. Instead, Lucifer had returned to his earlier whisper, only this time Archie was a man who could hear him clearly. "I am the source of all the darkness in this world. I am every agony in all who suffer. Every sickness, every infection of the flesh and spirit comes from me. Every corrupt politician and two- faced sociopath lives through me. I am the very evil in all terrible men."

Lucifer, it seemed, embraced his darkness. He chose not to love God or do good, but to despise God and do evil. Surely an omnipotent lord could have stripped him of the choice, but doing so would have eliminated genuine love at the same time. Forcing someone to love you was tyranny. Allowing them to hate you when you could destroy them, was true benevolence. God had turned the other cheek.

As though confirming his freedom of choice intact, Lucifer hushed tone returned to him once more.

"I am the leviathan"

Archie heard the beast before he saw it. It started

as a deep rumbling sounding in the distance, growing nearer like an approaching avalanche. Then it was there, a giant rogue wave racing towards him. As the wave formed a lip, its broken white crest seemed to smile, grinning like deadly rows of shark teeth.

All Archie could manage was, "Oh no" as though this might prepare his vessel in some way for the violent collision.

The Argo was heaved into the air and capsized, like it was nothing more than a toy in a child's bath. Archie struggled under the roiling water in a tangle of lines, unsure of his bearings as he was flipped over and over like as a sock in the dryer. He was only sure he was beneath the surface and when the water finally calmed he could discern a shape in the sunless sea. It was just light colored enough to be seen in the dark water, illuminated by the stars which breached the first fathom. A giant crucifix, turned upside down, the symbol of

Lucifer. Recognizing it as his mast which been turned into this evil symbol, he kicked towards the surface and his upside down vessel.

The sight that greeted him when he broke the surface was hardly better than the one below. His ship was drowning. The Argo's keel, a giant fin attached to the hull and filled with heavy lead, was pointing straight into the air. That keel normally served as a fin, cutting through the water as a counterforce to sail above which weaved through the wind as a wing, rather like a plane flying sideways. It was weighted precisely so that the boat could heel without tipping, and even if such a disaster occurred, it should have been able to regain itself. And yet Archie could discern that the keel was not righting the boat as designed, but was falling lower against the back drop of stars. It was sinking.

His knowledge of the Argo was carnal, and in his mind's eye he could envision the various points in his vessel where water was infiltrating the cabin, filling it and making it just heavier than the designer had accounted for in his calculations for a self-righting vessel. He saw the porthole with the leaky seal that always wept in the rain now spraying saltwater into the galley, while his automatic pumps fixed in the lowest part of the bilge hung useless above like broken chandeliers.

He sought for something buoyant to cling to among his items now strewn across the water and found the sea anchor, a yellow rubber bag that when opened would fill with water. It would not support his dense weight and would sink soon on its own, but it gave him a desperate idea. Wrapping the line of the bag once around his chest, he swam to the Argo, finding the main halyard line along the way and holding it in his teeth. Reaching the slippery black hull, he used the sharp barnacles affixed there to board his inverted craft, mounting the keel and straddling it with a leg on either side.

He tied the two lines to life he possessed as one, and tying the knot fast, tossed the open anchor bag into the sea. As it filled with water it brought the line draped over the keel in front of him taut. When the sea anchor sank deeper than the submerged masthead, the line tugged on the halyard fixed there, pulling the tip of the metal spar towards the surface.

Archie laughed with hope and glee as the minor extra weight of the anchor began to right his ship like the burdened half of scale. Hardly had the last sac of his lungs emptied in happy breath when the line, running hot with friction against the keel edge, began to unbraid and fray. He had only a second to react, snatching the line in either hand in the same instance it snapped into two under the heavy tonnage.

He became the fulcrum point, straining to hold the immense weight as the Argo renewed capsizing. At first, the descending anchor line ran through his clenched fist, but he willed himself to grip it tighter even though it cut into his flesh. He tried reflexively to release the burning braid, but he commanded it, "No! I am more than you, my flesh!" He pushed through the pain, which was not passive as it normally was, but rather one he forced himself to endure.

Only when a meter of line was stained red with blood did it finally relent its pace, halting and heaving its load upon Archie's limbs. The Argo was beginning to right itself now, only too slowly. Archie shouted through locked teeth over the tearing sound opined from his left shoulder. Still, he would not let go.

His eyes were closed in wincing torment so that he could not see that the Argo had begun to upright itself. Only when he and the keel entered the water once more did he release his hold, as the Argo's point of gravity suddenly shifted and the mast surfaced, rising once more to its apex.

CHAPTER THIRTY-TWO

His arm hung uselessly by its hinge the next day, but he was free of worry about how to repair it. He knew he had only to endure it. Instead, it was the Argo he sought to restore to function as he wrangled the engine back into alignment with the shaft which spun the propeller. One of the four brackets securing it had broken loose when it was tossed upside down, causing it to breach the deck cover above it which was now lost altogether. He worked with a halyard and winch to shift the block to its proper place in the hold now exposed in front of the helm.

The urea in the sweat that spilled from his brow stung his eyes, causing him to break in order to tie a dirty rag around his skull like a headband. When the perspiration cleared from his eyes, he noticed a pair of dorsal fins carving the water towards his injured vessel. He was as sure that he was in the Mediterranean as he was that no sharks roamed those waters. Yet they were there. Plucking a can of chili floating in the water in the engine compartment, he pitched it at the approaching predators which broke their formation in retreat.

"I'm not for you, you dumb fuckin' fish," he spat, knowing them for their true form. Lucifer, he was sure he would never see again. Satan would not waste more effort on him, seeking instead to ply his tricks on a less suspecting soul. These sharks were as demons, too simple to know better. Only as they fled from him did he finally understand what it meant to abolish all evil from his life. Only here, at the end of his, did he truly manage it. He had looked to God to defend him from it, but instead of giving him a shield, he was passed a sword. He thought the hate learned in war was a doorway to sin, but last night he had confronted it in its purest form, denouncing it, and it doing so, he became a man who did not fear evil. Evil feared him.

He wished it would have happened sooner in his life, but perhaps this was how it was always meant to be. He had been graduated through increasingly larger challenges throughout his existence, all so that he could surmount this one: the realization that evil was a coward. A foe vanquished by truth and obliterated by faith, an allegiance to good.

Still, he knew he was not done. There was a final test before him, carried on the back of the advancing storm clouds already pelting him with deliberate rain zeroed precisely for him, as though each drop was kamikaze piloted, hell bent on mutual destruction against his skin. He worked feverishly to reconnect the shaft to the engine as the precipitation plummeted around him. His sails had survived the rollover intact, but Archie knew the low pressure which bore those clouds towards him were winds which could not be traveled by sail alone.

He had no doubt that the inbound deluge was meant for him. The flood was coming and his body was the Ark. The memories came to him now, two by two to depart this world. Meaghan was among them and to see her again he felt many years had passed between them already. Time was relative, and he was traveling towards his destiny at an accelerated rate, each day a full turn around the sun. She had stayed beautiful in his mind, not aged a single minute, but he had grown old.

Using his one good arm, he grabbed the binnacle to pull himself out of the engine compartment. Sitting behind the wheel, he turned the ignition which answered with the harsh squealing of metal on metal as the shaft spun on its new and haphazard axis. Even as he plugged one ear and leaned over the helm to inspect the viability of his repair below, the noise abated as the metal scored in the right places.

His sails were already up, for having raised them for inspection, he let them luff uselessly while he worked. All he had to do now was spin the wheel hard to port until the strong and growing breeze snared the canvas, tugging the Argo away.

CHAPTER THIRTY-THREE

One of his first missions was a security detail in the jungles of Panama escorting a group of engineers who were building schools for the locals. Still young and curious, he wandered off on his own into the thick canopy weaving a machete before him, more to catch the strands of spider webs than to cut vegetation from his path. He became aware of the presence of a few large primates, hidden somewhere in the thick vegetation. He could not see them, but the low tones they exchanged with each other gave them away. He proceeded unconcerned, taking little notice that the grunts and calls had doubled, then tripled as he trekked deeper and deeper into their home. Only when they unanimously sounded the alarm with shrill cries and wild, primitive incantations did he realize he was an outnumbered intruder trespassing on their territory. He withdrew his pistol as the shrubbery shook and shuddered all around him, the angry apes cordoning off the invader. At first he only walked back the way he came, but it soon became apparent that was not fast enough for the defenders closing in, so he sprinted towards safety, the apes escorting him all the while they jeered and threatened, daring him to slow his pace.

The ocean tossed and heaved waves so immense, it would have been difficult for anyone in the vicinity to see the little sailboat struggling through them. As the Argo careened through the storm, which had arrived in full force shortly after nightfall, he felt once more pursued and heckled by the beasts of nature. He had wandered once more into a realm where he was not welcome. The wind screamed at him while three story waves surrounded him, jostling him to and fro. Only this time he would not turn back, towards the safety of man. His destination was beyond man, animal or nature and he would not be intimidated again. He crashed through wave after wave, cleaving each in two as they continued to march upon him like inexhaustible ranks of troops determined to halt his advance.

He divided his attention between the helm and a project he had devised against the incoming swells, working to pour a mixture olive oil and transmission fluid into a pair of gallon sized plastic jugs. The lurching of his vessel made the task difficult, and nearly as much oil coated the deck as fell into the bottles. The nausea from the lurching was intense, causing him to vomit but he continued his work without wiping the bile from his mouth. Capping the containers off, he connected their necks with a long string which he draped over his own so that his hands could be free as he half-crawled to the bow. He lifted the lazarette, a small cubby where the anchor line was stowed, and sat in it with his knees to his chest so that he might not be thrown from the pitching bow. Using the tip of his knife, he punched a few small holes in each bottle before draping them over his prow, so that one swung from either side of his bow, like the dripping hunks of blubber whalers once hung to calm stormy seas threatening their ship. Like the mariners before him, he did not know the science of it, only that it had worked for some and it may for him.

Emboldened by his own cleverness and made hysterical by the overwhelming altitude of the incredible swells, he challenged the aggravated sea around him.

"Come on! Is that all you've got? I'm here! Fight me! You're not the first menstruating bitch I've known!"

As though in reply, a large wave crashed over the deck, ripping Archie from the binnacle. When it at last washed over the side, he found himself clinging to a lifeline with his sole usable arm. He regained the helm humbled, like a child whose temper tantrum was crushed by the superior wrath of a parent. As he lashed himself to the wheel, he muttered, "Touché, Mademoiselle."

He leaned over the helm to inspect the exposed engine churning below, ensuring the compartment had not filled with water despite the heavy rain, a sign that his bilge pump was working steadily. Normally he might have heard the pump whirr and spit water overboard, but the howling wind masked all low decimal noise.

Every passing wave lifted his stern so high his rudder and propeller were raised out of the water, and for those helpless moments, he lost all steerage and headway. As soon as the aft fell back into the sea, he had to rally his vessel back on a course avoiding the next side broaching swell.

He was curiously noting that the metal cables supporting the mast were emitting a low, intensifying buzz as they vibrated like a string on a violin when an explosion sounded just off his stern and for pause he was both blind and deaf. The burnt air reeked of ozone as it had once during his last deployment when an airstrike intended for the enemy had nearly incinerated him. Before he could imagine what had occurred, it happened again just off his bow as a brilliant white bolt shot into the water with such intensity the surface erupted into flames that burned and steamed decimated particles. He looked at the giant metal mast in front of him and shook his head in an attempt to forget the fourth grade lesson about Franklin, a kite and a key.

Less water seemed to be washing over his deck now, and he could discern some amelioration of the sea as the olive oil poured from the bottles, trailing behind like let blood. Still, he knew it would not be enough, for spilt blood only wetted savage appetites.

Lightening continued to erupt nearby, each time proceeded by the charging of the air which strummed his mast as the wind tripled in force, raking over the vessel from stern to bow. It hurt him to hear each violent snap of his sails which answered to every successive blow dealt by the gale. Bracing himself, he clutched the wheel he was strapped to as this tempest whipped his ship, like flogs upon his own back.

When one of the metal cables securing the top of the mast to the deck snapped under the force, it was as if the rib nearest his heart had been broken. He suffered even greater when his foresail tore under the thrashing, shuddering as though it was his own skin which was split. The sail screamed as it was shredded to tethers and tape until it was silenced by a lightning strike off the bow, so near and fierce it supercharged the surrounding air with heat and energy, catching the mangled canvas on fire.

Archie watched in horror as the flames jumped to his mainsail, crawling towards the base of the sail and boom which swung only a foot away from his head. He tried to untie the knot securing him to wheel so that he might hide from the flames licking his face, but in his previous haste he tied a foul knot, fast and with no easy release. He could only bury his face inside his shirt, coughing up the smoke which threatened to choke him. Working blind, he thumbed open his pocket knife and sawed desperately at the line detaining him, but failed for the blade was dull and the line was stronger when wet.

He uncovered his face when the heat abated and in its place a terrible cold arrived. He shivered in the frosty temperature which had come suddenly, as though carried on the backs of the monstrous swells which rushed forward, dwarfing his previous tormentors.

And then it was there before him. His destiny, racing towards him like a long separated friend. He had to tilt his head back to take in the full, insurmountable height of the towering wave erecting before him. He knew what waited for him atop that watery mount, and that there was no farther height above it that he could ever climb and still remain a member of the physical world. It was his Golgotha, a mountain of skull and bones waiting for him.

As the Argo met this rogue wave its bow raised high above the stern, pitching like a plane leaving the tarmac. At this angle the propeller found full submersion, digging steadily in the water. He pushed the motor harder than he had ever before, knowing he was damaging it beyond repair. Burnt oil spurt from the hot and melting gaskets of the engine case, spraying his face in the crude smut. It whined like a neighing horse in protest, billowing toxic black plumes. Still, he urged the old combustible to churn forth, willing it towards its own destruction. Its pistons pumped furiously to meet his demand, like a convulsing heart compressing blood. Archie clung to the wheel to keep the line binding him from digging into his back as the Argo pointed almost straight up, tools and belongings slipping down the deck and disappearing behind him. He felt queasy as his stomach fell back against his spine and prayed the decrepit diesel could hold out just a moment more, for if it failed now the Argo would slide down the wave which would flip the boat end over end.

The mast was naked of the sails and charred black by their incineration. As Archie beheld it, the monstrous wave before him seemed less important. He embraced that mast, for now, in his mind, it was no longer the spar, but a giant, heavy crucifix which he carried towards his fate. He moved the throttle lever the last minor fraction that remained in play, giving the Argo a boost which pushed it over the lip of the wave and upon the peak an instant before the engine squealed and shattered apart.

For a serene moment, the boat leveled on the top of the wave. Archie looked about him, finally high above the sea which had tormented, ridiculed and mocked him, trying to destroy him but succeeding only in raising him to this amazing height. He felt something like laughter in his chest, a pleasant pressure on his bosom but he emitted no sound for he had suddenly reached a condition where emotion was experienced beyond his body, independent and free of its convulsions.

He saw a time, before Meaghan, sitting in his car and feeling happy and loved. He wanted to say, "I love you too" but there was no one in the passenger seat so the sentiment would have gone unheard. It made him feel lonely to have no one to deliver the warm sentiment to, but now he realized his folly. He was not alone in that car. He had only to return the love. God had been with him, always. God had thought of him, constantly and with great care. God was a spring, always flowing, always giving. God loved him.

Then the moment was over. The wave beneath

him broke, but gently and like an elevator in a nice hotel, it lowered him while at the same time the water that had been its foundation rose above him into an even grander breaker which fell over the Argo, burying it deep in the basement of the sea.

Archie was only dimly aware of his ingurgitation into this belly. The waters calmed quickly after. Before it had roiled and kicked like a petulant baby, but now it was content, having been fed. Its meal devoured, the sea slept, returning to the equanimity it had before the storm.

The Argo was gone.

CHAPTER THIRTY-FOUR

The sun was beaming onto the granules of sand that formed the beach, nourishing it with light waves as food heats the body. It was a quite shore, undisturbed by the foot print of man, excepting the battered craft which was beached on its side. Seagulls perched on the wreckage as though claiming the apparently abandoned craft. They jaunted into flight with alarm as a sudden commotion sounded within.

The hatch scraped open and Archie emerged, dazed by the blinding sun and disorientated by a steady underfoot, devoid of the familiar rocking current. He shoved aside debris that blockaded the hatchway, driftwood, seaweed and his broken helm. Careful of his bare feet, he climbed gingerly though the boats carnage to disembark.

He trudged wearily down the beach, resisting the inclination to survey his beached craft. He had an idea of her disposition but not the heart to witness it. She was like an ex-girlfriend who had degraded herself and it hurt him to know he might have saved her had he stayed a closer course.

He wondered where he was walking to, trying to find some useful reference as a landmark. The answer came to him in three gentle taps on his shoulder, a signal he knew from his victories in the cage. He had had won, for this was Greece and it embraced him like a shiny belt around his waist. He could simply feel it to be so. It was surreal, like returning home from his first deployment to a place that was both strange and familiar all at once.

His excitement was doubled by his solitude, for he could express it in total confidence. He ran down the shoreline, splashing through the lapping waves which, having attacked so viciously just hours ago, now rushed forward to kiss his feet and pay homage. His torn shirt, which clung to him only by a fragment around his neck, he tore from his shoulders, for even a regal cape could not adorn him as well as his own broad back which had served him through his voyage and made him king of the seas.

He was elated to have soil beneath his feet, and fell to his knees so that he could scoop it up and clutch it to his bosom, fulfilling the heartfelt longing he had felt to have it so near the night before. Still, he was surprised that it didn't feel like new territory trodden, as much as a return.

This quandary was cut short when he heard movement behind him and had the instinct, passed to him from an earlier edition of man who lived hunted by beasts, that an animal was approaching from the rear and at full speed. He tried to rise and turn at the same time but had not made it off his knees when the wild thing leaped on his chest, planting paws on his sternum.

Archie had closed his eyes at the moment of impact, such that he felt the moist, hot breath upon his face before he beheld the creature. The smell was familiar to him, firing neurons in his brain that had not been triggered since he was boy. When he opened his eyes, he beheld the adorably ugly face of his childhood bulldog.

"Chopper!"

His exclamation was returned by the furious wiggling of the dog's hindquarters, a motion to compensate for the lack of a full length tail to wag. Archie knew it was a dream, one which had visited him before. The last time this dream visited him, he tried to kiss the dog and woke when his lips pressed against the bulkhead. He grasped the dog's loose skin and pulled him close in an attempt to hang on to his pet as long as he could, dreading the inevitable departure of a return to reality, another collision with a wall.

The excited canine ceased his frantic wiggling

so that his boyhood master could hold him better, as though knowing this is what was needed. Archie buried his face in the soft fur of the dog's neck, inhaling the scent while remembering a blanket he had as toddler, one he could never sleep without. He used to hold it in his fist while sucking his thumb so that the corner of the blanket was pressed under his nose, the aroma itself a comforting quilt. As he clutched his dog, he seemed to recall every hard moment of his life since that blanket.

As he inhaled deeply, he felt the full weight of every sorrow and loss he had ever suffered make a final, light impression on him, as though each took the form of a small sparrow, and each in turn landed on his shoulder to remind him of their encounter, before fluttering off and leaving him forever. As he sobbed into the dog's clean coat, the elation he felt as his burdens abandoned him was overwhelming, for all that remained within him was every instance of joy and happiness he had ever known.

When he opened his eyes, the world around him was new again, as it had not been since his infancy. Everything, from the sky above to the ground below, was such a miracle that the presence of his long departed dog no longer stood out as unusual.

When he saw he a stranger approaching in the distance, he was not worried who it might be, or any potential threat he might pose. It was not only that he had conquered hell and its master, but that he once again possessed the childlike assurance that all those in this world were good.

"*Yasou, Popou,*" Archie said, hailing his grandfather.

"You remembered the Greek I spoke," Popou answered.

"I remember everything you ever said," he returned, and that was the last time he ever spoke. There was no longer a need for speech between him and his grandfather, for they understood one another entirely and perfectly.

Archie took a final look at the immense ocean he had crossed, only now his eyes seemed to see without end, and he could sight across it to behold Meaghan. She was in a fit of nostalgia, strolling the docks at the marina, trying to remember him.

He smiled that this ocean was now a puddle, a matter of a space and time he could cross in the span it took to blink. So he blinked, returning to her like a message in a bottle, inhabiting a space she could not yet fit. She received his words without the middleman letters on paper would have been and she felt comforted. She knew he was not gone. He was waiting. She saw herself in the handlebar mirror of his motorcycle, just over his shoulder, as he was telling her to just enjoy the ride.

As Archie and Popou embraced, more figures

approached from all around, enveloping them and welcoming him. Wordlessly.

A Personal Message from Author

A sincere thank you for reading my novel! I hope you enjoyed it. Please email me so we can discuss life and I can add you to my mailing list to offer you future discounts, sneak peeks and immediate notices of release for my upcoming works. You can do so at

contact@authortakisjpepe.org

I would also like to take this opportunity to direct other writers to the many talents of Donna Carbone, a managing director at the Burt Reynolds Institute for Theatre in Jupiter, Florida.

http://writeforyoullc.com

And Jennifer Jansen of Melbourne, Australia, an excellent proof reader and editor whose abilities were of great contribution to this work.

ljenniferjansen@gmail.com

ABOUT THE AUTHOR

Takis John Pepe is a U.S. Air Force veteran who has served in combat operations in Iraq and Afghanistan, a former amateur cage fighter, a professional mariner, graduate of Nova Southeastern University and National Security expert.